THE TROUBLEMAKER

CATHRYN FOX

COPYRIGHT

The Troublemaker

ISBN Ebook: 978-1-989374-24-5
ISBN Print: 978-1-989374-23-8

CASON

I nudge my best bud Cole as he lifts his near empty beer bottle to his lips. "Who's the cute girl with Kinsley?" I ask and take in the hot blonde shaking her ass on stage, as our good friend Kinsley dances wildly beside her. Kinsley, with her bright pink hair and numerous piercings, never fails to stand out in a crowd. I always liked the way she marched to the beat of her own drum. The saying is cliché, I know, but confidence radiates off her, and her refusal to cave to the ridiculous societal pressures put on women has always impressed me.

Cole takes a long pull from the bottle, and he scans the Vegas nightclub. "You mean the cute blonde?" His gaze rakes over our eclectic group of friends as they butcher some Neil Diamond song, giving zero fucks that my ears are bleeding from the off-key notes.

But I'm glad they're all having fun with the karaoke machine. That's what weddings in Vegas are all about, right? Tomorrow our friend Rider—aka the Wingman—and his gorgeous fiancée Jules will be tying the knot. I couldn't be happier, but that doesn't mean I'm going to get up on that stage and make a fool of myself like everyone else in the wedding party.

My younger sister Nina—Cole's wife—takes the microphone, and things go from bad to worse. I must have done something shitty in a past lifetime to be subjected to this kind of torture. Cole cringes and turns my way.

"Sweet baby Jesus. Don't tell her I said this, but she needs to stick to her day job," he says.

I laugh at that. My sister is a New York Times bestselling author, and the love of my best friend's life. I smile, because she looks happy and all I've ever wanted was for her to have the life she deserves—with a guy who knows her value, and knows how to treat a woman with respect. The two have been happily married for a few years now, and after a successful NHL season, this break away from work and their two kids looks good on them both.

"Do you know who she is?" I ask again as the blonde looks my way.

"She's a friend of Jule's and Kinsley's. I think all three of them go way back. I can't remember her name. Maybe it's Emma or something. Why, you like her?" he asks.

A trio of barely dressed women in heels so high it's a wonder their noses aren't bleeding, giggle and stare as they walk by our table—obviously trying to get our attention. The people in the club went a little wild when half of the Seattle Shooter's team sauntered in. The staff quickly quieted them, but many have been trying to crash our private party.

I smile at them as they pass. "She's cute and fun. What's not to like?"

Cole nods and takes another pull from his beer. "She's definitely your type. Then again, who isn't?"

"Hey," I say and push him. The server comes by with a couple of fresh beers and sets them in front of us. "Can I get you boys anything else?" she asks as she drops a napkin in front of me, her name and number scribbled on it.

"We're good for now."

"Okay, just shout if you need anything." She offers me a big smile. "I do mean anything."

I nod, and she saunters off, an extra little shake in her backside.

"Are you denying that every woman is your type?" Cole asks when it's just the two of us.

"Well yeah...I mean...no. I just like women." It's true I do, although I have to say I am so goddamn played out these days, it's killing me. I'd love to go to bed with the same woman every night, and more importantly, wake up with her every morning. Too bad settling down just isn't in my future —and it's not because I'm commitment phobic.

"And they like you," he says, nodding to the napkin in front of me. "Obviously, but someday though, the right one will come along, and once you fall in love, your priorities will change big time. Next thing you know, your ride will be a minivan and a stroller."

I shrug, not worried about trading in the sports car— because I want that. Cole is my best friend, and on some level, he must know I want what he has, but it's out of my reach. What is it women say about me? Emotionally closed off? Yeah, that's it. It's no secret that two weeks is my limit with a woman. I thought things might go further a couple years back when I hooked up with Jess, my sister's best friend. But nope, I couldn't seem to give her what she wanted, and she dumped me for a guy who could express himself better than me.

Love and affection were rare things in my household growing up, which might be why it's hard for me to express myself. I usually just fuck things up and end up hurting whoever I'm with. I've since learned that if I bail after two weeks, no one falls in love, no one gets hurt. I'm just glad Nina never had the same problem, and is now in a loving relationship with my buddy.

"No minivan for me," I say and casually stretch my legs out, pretending I'm relaxed when I'm actually strung so tight my shoulders are practically hugging my ears. I should probably get laid tonight, it's what I always do to take my mind off things, but I'm not even sure if I want to have sex. If I tell Cole that I might just go to bed alone, he'll check me in to the nearest clinic. "I'm a bachelor for life," I add.

Cole makes a sound, one that suggests I'm full of shit, and says, "I think it'll happen when you least expect it, and with the last person you expect it to happen with."

I lift my bottle and tip it his way. "Look at that. My best friend. The hockey player and a philosopher. God, I'm a lucky guy."

"Fuck off," he says and shoves me. "I'm right. You'll see."

I snort. "Want to bet?"

He glances around, the overhead strobe lights beginning to give me a headache. "We are in Vegas. I'll take that bet."

I shake my head. "Nah, forget it."

"Forget what?" Nina asks, as she comes our way, and sets herself on Cole's lap. She runs her hands through his hair, and kisses him like her brother isn't sitting there watching the two display affection. While I'd rather not watch them make out, my heart swells, happy and envious at what they have.

"Jesus, get a room already," I say.

She grins at me. "Ooh, that's a good idea. What were you two talking about?" she asks.

Cole opens his mouth, but I lean forward and cut him off. "That girl dancing with Kinsley. Do you know her?"

She turns. "Yeah, that's Jules's friend. She's here for the wedding, too. Her name is Emily."

"Emma. Emily. I was close," Cole says, and I roll my eyes at him.

"She asked about you," Nina says and takes Cole's beer.

My dick twitches. "Oh yeah."

She takes a big drink of beer, leaving me hanging. "Thanks babe," she says and hands the bottle back to Cole. She lifts her head to see me as she wipes her mouth with the back of her hand. "Yeah, but I told her to stay away." She tucks a strand of hair behind her ear. "I let her know you were nothing but trouble."

"Sis, seriously. When did little Neaner Neaner become such a cock blocker?" I ask, using the childhood nickname she hates, just to piss her off.

Cole nearly spews a mouthful of beer. "Watch what you're calling my wife, buddy."

Nina lifts her chin an inch, all tough with her husband backing her up, and my lips twitch. "That's right, Cason. Talk to me like that again, and Cole will put a beating on you."

I laugh, and Cole grins. The last fight we had—over Nina —I blackened his eye and they both know it. They don't call me Crazy Callaghan the Troublemaker—on and off the ice— for nothing.

"Cool it you two," Cole says. "Everyone is coming back."

The gang are all laughing and hanging off each other as they come back to the big round table. Rider orders a round of shots for us all. They come and we lift them in salute. Kane, Rider's best friend—his brother—lifts his glass.

"To Rider and Jules," he says and we all down our tequila and reach for a lime from the bowl in the center. My hand connects with Emily's and she gives me a smile.

"Here," she says, and puts the lime in my mouth. I suck on it, and she nibbles on her bottom lip as she watches me. Yeah, maybe if I took her to bed, it would help me forget about all the things I want, but can never have. Juice drips down my chin, and I grab the napkin to wipe it.

"Uh oh," she says, dark lashes fluttering over blue eyes.

"What?"

She points to the napkin. "I think you smudged the number."

I shrug. "I wasn't interested anyway."

Her lips pucker as she reaches into her purse. "Maybe you'll be interested in this," she says, and discreetly slides her room key into my hand. I shift and shove it into my back pocket for safe keeping.

Kinsley grabs my hand. "Come on, Cason. You are not sitting here all night."

"I am not singing," I groan in protest.

"Fine, then you can dance with me. This is Vegas baby. You've been doing nothing but mope since we got here."

"I am not..." I let my words fall off because it's possible she's right. She pulls me from my chair, and the second I stand, asshole and fellow teammate Liam, drops into my chair and turns his focus to Emily.

Motherfucker.

Where the hell is bro code? We don't hit on another guy's woman. Not that Emily is my woman. She's not. But still, I was just sitting with her, and Liam is breaking bro code rules. I shake my head. I guess that's why his on ice handle is the Rule Breaker, and I should probably cut him some slack; he recently lost his dad, and there was a huge scandal, and has been drinking steadily since arriving. I'm a bit worried about his mental state to be honest. I'm glad he's here with us this weekend. I think he needs his friends around.

Kinsley drags me onto the dance floor just as those working the karaoke machine change to a slow song. I pull her into my arms, and her sweet vanilla scent fills my senses. I put my nose to her hair and breathe her in.

"Did you just smell me?" she asks.

"Why do you always smell so good?" I ask.

She laughs, and the sound curls around me. "Because I own a food truck. No matter how many times I shower I still smell like street tacos."

"You think you smell like street tacos?" I chuckle at that.

"Yeah, I've been thinking of bottling the scent. Talk about an aphrodisiac for men, huh? They'd be coming at me from miles."

I put my hands on her hips as she sways. What the fuck? Is that my dick twitching? Yeah, maybe I really am in bad shape if my dick is standing up and taking notice. Not that Kinsley isn't hot, it's just that she and I are friends. We go way back, and I eat at her food truck every chance I get.

My dick should not be moving.

"First, you smell like cupcakes, and second you don't need to smell like a taco to attract a guy, Kins. I'm sure they're lining up for you."

She snorts and looks at me like I have a brain tumor. "Oh, they're lining up all right. I own a food truck remember?"

Wait, does she think that's the only reason a man would be interested in her? Fuck, she's hot with her wild pink hair and numerous piercings, not to mention the abundance of curves any guy would be lucky to sink his teeth into. She's completely different from the puck bunnies who line up to meet us after a game, but that's why I like her. Like I said, she marches to the beat of her own drum and cares little about social norms.

A round of cheers erupt from behind us as the gang all do another shot. This time Liam is putting a lime to Emily's lips and she sidles closer to him. He can flirt with her all he wants. I'm the one with her room key in my back pocket. I'm just not sure I want to use it. Maybe all this pumped in oxygen is messing with my brain.

"You like her, huh?" Kinsley asks, and lowers her head. While I can't see her expression, I hear a hint of dejection in her voice. I must be mistaken. Why would she be upset that I liked her friend? Before I can say anything, she says, "She likes you, too, Cason. Then again, who doesn't?"

"Are you saying you like me, Kins," I tease. "You think I'm a big fat snack you'd like to bite into?"

Her face crinkles like she'd just tasted something sour. "And my snacking stops today," she says with a laugh.

She's a joker, a teaser, but for some reason those words hit like a punch. I smile to hide the blow and say, "Always good to know where I stand with the ladies."

"I'm not one of your ladies, I'm your friend, and you're welcome," she says. "But you should go for it with Emily. She's always looking for a good time, and has no desire to get serious. She's having too much fun being single I guess."

"You two go way back?"

"Friends since childhood. She stuck by me when I quit law school and bought a truck."

"She sounds like a good friend."

"She is." She arches a brow, but there is something I don't recognize in her eyes. It can't be jealousy. She just told me she was off snacking. "Are you going to go for it?"

I shrug. One because I'm unsure and two it feels weird talking to Kinsley about this. But maybe she's right. Maybe I should stop feeling sorry for myself and hook up with a girl who knows where I stand. We break apart as the song ends. She saunters off, her swaying ass dragging my focus, and teasing something deep inside me. My dick twitches again.

What the ever loving fuck is going on with me?

Am I really upset that I'm not her type, that she doesn't want to crawl between the sheets with me? I mean, that's good though, right? That should make me happy.

We're friends for God's sake.

I shouldn't want to sleep with her. Shouldn't all of a sudden be thinking about her lush body beneath mine. I shut down my brain, and redirect my train of thoughts to ones that don't involve my friend naked.

Too bad my dick didn't get the memo.

2

KINSLEY

"How did you end up with the honeymoon suite anyway?" Emily asks me, as I practically carry her to my bed, and toss her on it. She widens her arms and makes snow angels on my big, inviting mattress. She's a hot mess, and if she could see herself, she'd be mortified. As a cosmetologist, she's always so well put together. Tequila is not her friend.

"I guess I just got lucky," I say. The hotel had lost my reservation, so they put me in one of their posh honeymoon suites. I'm not about to complain. The place is bigger than my Seattle condo.

"This bed is big enough to sleep six," she tells me.

It's true it is, but I wish I was sleeping alone in it, left to my thoughts about Cason, and the way his body moved with mine. Yeah, I want to lay here alone and fantasize, but I won't. Not with Emily next to me. She's had far too much tequila, and I needed to make sure she landed in bed safely. Friends take care of each other. She insisted she needed to go to her room, although she couldn't remember why, and when her key was nowhere to be found, taking her here to my big suite to sleep off the tequila was a no-brainer.

"Wait," she says and sits up. She peels her tongue from the roof of her mouth, and furrows her brow in thought. "I think I'm supposed to get lucky tonight."

I shake my head. "The only luck you're going to have is if you don't end up with your head in the toilet bowl." I gesture for her to lift her arms. "Come on, let me help you undress."

"That was good tequila," she says and I laugh as I peel her shirt off. She flops onto her pillow and I remove her pants, leaving her in her bra and panties. I help her between the sheets and put a big glass of water on the nightstand. As she drifts off, I brush my teeth, and I'm about to undress and climb in beside her, but stop short when she starts snoring so hard, the walls begin to vibrate around me.

"Oh, hell no!"

I grab her purse and search for her key. Dammit. Would they give me a new one at the front desk, if I asked? If I had her ID, pretended to be her, what choice would they have? Even though we look nothing alike, I snatch her wallet from her purse, and head down to the front desk.

Jackpot.

Ten minutes later, I let myself into her room, and with exhaustion from a long day pulling at me, I strip off and collapse onto her bed. I close my eyes, and the second I do, visions of a naked Cason dance in my head. If I'm lucky, maybe I'll have another sex dream tonight, just like the ones I've been having for the past year now.

Last summer, Cason and a few of his buddies had been playing street hockey with some neighborhood kids, and they all showed up half naked, and fully starved. Something shifted in me that day, woke with a vengeance. I always knew he was smoking hot, but damn, my ovaries nearly exploded as he gave me an up close and personal view of his hard chest and tight six pack.

Would his lower body be just as hard?

Dammit.

I should not be fantasizing about my good friend, especially when he just showed interest in Emily. I lied when he asked if he was a big fat snack. Oh, did I ever lie. What I'd do to take a bite out of him. But Emily's the one he wants to go to bed with, not me—a tatted up girl who is the antithesis of the women who hang off his arm. I exhale sharply and work to push all images of Cason from my mind as I drift off. A long while later, a voice pulls me awake.

"Hey," Cason says.

I take a breath, and then another. What the hell is going on? I try to focus, but my room is too dark to see anything. A big callused hand touches my face, and that's when I clue in. I'm fantasizing about Cason again.

"Mmm," I say and settle against the pillow, ready to ride this dream out to orgasm. His lips find mine, and I moan into his mouth, to let him know how much I like his kisses, even if they're not real. No, none of this is tangible, not the weight of his body pressing down on mine, the hard cock indenting my leg, or the hungry groans that sound far too real.

"Sorry I took so long," he says, and I put my legs around him, and move my hips.

"Forgiven," I murmur and for a brief second he goes still. His body stiffens, and I'm not just talking about the anaconda between his legs. Oh, God, this is my dream, and I get to dictate what happens next, not him. I grip his hair, bring his mouth back to mine, and kiss the living hell out of him.

I lift my hips, grind against his body, and just give in to the things this man makes me feel. I'm not so sure I'd be so wild and bold in real life. It's true, my outward appearance tells a story, a rebellious daughter of lawyer parents, who was supposed to follow in their footsteps, but inside, I'm not always as confident as I let on. But this, in my dreams, I can let go, and take what I want.

"Cason," I murmur. "Get naked all ready." I tear at his T-shirt, needing his skin next to mine. He reaches over his back and tugs, removing the stupid piece of fabric that's preventing me from touching him all over. I can't see a thing, but that's okay. I want to feel my way around his luscious body anyway.

"Better?" he asks.

"Much," I say, as his hand goes to my breast. He kneads me in his big, hockey player palms, rough from years of handling the stick, his thumb brushing against my nipple and holy, it's all I can do not to come.

"Yes," I say. "Just like that."

I fist his hair and push on him, until his mouth is right where I want it to be—for now. Soon I'll want it between my quivering legs. He chuckles at my boldness, and the sound vibrates through my body, and stimulates my throbbing clit.

"This what you want?" he asks, before pulling my hard nipple into his mouth. My lips part in ecstasy but no sound comes. He clearly knows what his kisses are doing to me. How could he not? I'm like a writhing, overstimulated nymphomaniac beneath him.

But I don't care.

My sex pulses, and I'm so damn wet and needy, I'm sure I'm going to climax the second he touches me. Let's find out. I grip his hair harder, and direct his mouth to my pussy, and he moves slower than I'd like, peppering hot, open mouthed kisses to my tingling stomach. He finally settles between my legs, and I arch up to meet his mouth.

The second his hot, wet tongue touches me, I let loose an agonized wail. "Yes," I cry out. He licks me, circles his tongue around my clit, and I grip the sheets and tug. "You are so good at that," I say. He should be. He's been with enough women, but this is my dream, and he's probably performing better because I'm the one directing the show. No one could be this skilled in real life, right?

I move shamelessly against his face, rub my pussy all over him and his moans of want encourage me all the more.

"Yeah, that's it. Take what you want," he says from deep between my legs. He inserts a finger into me, and my muscles clench as deep pleasure radiates from my core.

"God, yes," I say as he licks my clit and circles the hot bundle of nerves inside me. I move against him as he fucks me with his finger, sliding a second in for a snug fit, and I let go of the sheets and go up on my elbows. I can't see his face, so I close my eyes to imagine it as he takes me higher and higher until I'm soaring without wings.

"I'm...coming," I say and clench around his finger, so hard, it steals the breath from my lungs. My God, I've climaxed in my sleep dreaming of him before, but this is different. Far more intense. He pets me lightly, bringing me down to earth and before I can fully catch my breath, he stands to remove his pants.

The hiss of his zipper fills the silence of the room and I go up on all fours, to follow the sound. I moan, and breathe in his scent.

"I want you in my mouth," I say and he groans.

"Where are you?" he asks.

I sit on the edge of the bed and reach for him. My hand connects with his stomach. "Right here, waiting for you to put this big cock into my mouth."

"Fuck," he growls, and my hand slides lower to grasp his cock. I rub him lightly. Velvet wrapped around hard steel. As I stroke, he steps closer.

"You're going to choke me with this thing," I say, and he draws in a fast breath.

"I won't hurt you."

Cason is one badass motherfucker—most guys know not to mess with him—but underneath it all, he's sweet. I always knew that about him, which must be why his tenderness has worked its way into my dream. He's not the flowery prose kind of guy, and I've never really seen him display affection to any woman other than his sister, but I'm not asking for that at the moment.

"My mouth is open, Cason. Feed me your cock, and maybe I want it to hurt a bit."

He swallows, and I move forward so he can find my mouth. He grunts and taps my bottom lip. I lick him, taste the come dripping from his slit, and my moan seems to do something to him. He comes closer, and slides to the back of my throat. I relax my throat, take him deeper than I've ever taken any man and he thickens even more.

He grips my hair, wraps it around his hand, and follows the motion of my bobbing head. God, I've never much been into giving oral sex, but I like it with him. Everything from the way he tastes, to the groans crawling out of his throat turn me on even more.

"It's too good," he murmurs and pulls out of me.

"Then why stop?" I ask, my heart pounding as I squeak in a breath.

"I want to fuck you."

"Yeah, I want that, too."

More sounds fill the space between us; clothes rustling, foil ripping, and latex being rolled on.

"Middle of the bed," he demands in a soft voice.

"Ooh, I love it when you go all alpha like that," I say with a laugh.

"Yeah?"

"Yeah. I'm in the middle of the bed, now," I inform him.

"Legs spread?"

I widen my thighs in invitation. "All spread."

"Pussy wet?"

"Ah, yeah."

"Touch yourself. Let me know for sure."

I slide my hand down my body and moan when I find myself slippery wet. My God, I am so aroused, I'm ready to climax again. I roll my finger over my swollen clit, and I quiver from head to toe.

"Soaked," I murmur.

"Jesus, I wish I could fucking see you touching yourself." His breathing changes, becomes rough and labored. Is he visualizing me touching myself? Does that turn him on? "Hands above your head," he commands in a soft voice.

Ooh, that's different. I reach up and grip the rails. "Hands are exactly where you want them," I say.

The bed dips as he climbs on, and slides over me. "You want my cock?"

"Yesss," I hiss, as his lips crash over mine and muffle the sound. He kisses me hard, deeply, like a man who's been deprived of human contact. His hands touch me all over, slide up and down my arms, stroke my face, and shape my sides. His fingers move to my breasts, and he brushes the underside as I kiss him back, and savor the sweet taste of him, as our tongues play. His full weight presses me deeper into the mattress, and he shifts, his cock probing my opening.

I put my legs around him and lift my hips. "Please," I beg. "I need you to fuck me."

"You need to come, again?"

"God, you have no idea how much I want to come again."

He slides a hand between our bodies, and inches a thick finger into me. "I have a bit of an idea," he says with a chuckle.

I move against his finger as his thick cock indents my thigh. "I don't think I'm the only one who needs to come."

"You're right."

"Then please put you—"

Before I can finish the sentence he powers into me, driving so high and deep, I swear to God, my back teeth just rattled. He hits my cervix, and holy hell I almost climax again.

"This what you want?" he asks, and goes still, his cock stretching me in glorious ways.

"God, yes," I cry out, and nip at his shoulder and ear. He'd have a little bruise on both those places tomorrow—if this was real.

He grunts and pulls back. I cry as he almost slips free but then he pistons back inside me. I gasp. No man, not that I've been with a lot, has ever hit me so deeply before. He does it repeatedly, sliding past my G-spot, and hitting my cervix with his crown as his pelvis stimulates my clit with each thrust. It's the perfect trifecta, but then his mouth leaves mine and he wraps those hot lips around my nipple. The second he does, I know I'm a goner. Lost. Down for the count. All pleasure centers in my core, and I completely submit to it.

My senses explode, like rockets blasting off into the night. I can't see, hear, or speak. I can only feel a full body orgasm that strips away every thought I'd ever had, allowing me to focus solely on the most intense pleasure I've ever experienced.

I wrap my arms around him, my sex clenching hard around his beautiful cock, as I curl in tight.

"Jesus," he whispers as he holds me in a possessive way, absorbing the waves crashing over me. My body finally stops spasming, and I move my hips, wanting more...everything.

He jerks his hips forward, changing the rhythm and pace as he chases his own orgasm, and I hold him tight. "Yes," I say.

His breathing changes, and he buries his face in my neck,

kissing and sucking on my skin, like we're teenagers partaking in a hickey fest. Not that I ever did that. Much.

"I'm right there."

"I want to feel it," I say, and let loose a cry at his first sweet pulse. He goes still deep inside me, his body damp, his muscles rolling beneath my fingers. He spasms and pulses and grunts as he depletes himself, and I love all the real, honest, raw sex noises he's making. There is definitely nothing flowery about this man.

He finally stops and his lips find mine. His kisses are softer now, less hurried, and I melt against his tenderness.

"You good?" he asks.

"How could I not be good? Best. Sex. Ever."

He laughs at that, and inches out of me. "Really?"

I exhale a contented breath and roll to my side. He slides in behind me, the big spoon to my little one. "Of course. How could it not be? I'm dreaming."

3

CASON

What the ever loving fuck?

I just had the best sex of my life with Kinsley, and this whole time she thought she was dreaming? I hug her body to mine, her warm scent washing over me as her breathing slows, changes. As she falls asleep my brain zaps to life, trying to figure out what the hell just happened.

Okay, I came to this room expecting to find Emily, but the second Kinsley spoke, I knew it was her. I was ready to scream "abort" and run for the hills, until she wrapped her arms around me and devoured my mouth with hers, letting me know exactly how she wanted to play this mistake out. Although it sure didn't feel like a mistake.

Still, it was, and the right thing would have been to put a stop to it, but her body was so goddamn warm, and lush, and I'm just a simple man at heart—driven by baser needs. When she wrapped her legs around me, there wasn't a single man on the face of this earth with enough willpower to walk away from that.

Am I right, or am I right?

But what I'm supposed to do next is beyond me. I don't normally do sleepovers, but this is Kinsley I'm holding. My good *friend*, Kinsley—who was in some semi-sleep state while we had the most incredible, mind blowing sex in the dark of the night.

Do I stay?

Do I bail?

Do I pretend this never happened and we laugh it off come morning? Oh, yeah, how funny would this be: *Hey Kins, I came in here to fuck Emily, but found you instead, and you know me, any warm body will do.*

I hardly think she'd find that laughable. I certainly don't.

Jesus. I don't want her to think she was nothing more than a warm body for me—that's fucking demeaning and wrong. I have a reputation sure, but I don't for one second want her to think none of this meant anything. The honest to God's truth is she *was* my first choice, but I walked away from that because of our friendship.

Which now could be in jeopardy. Could be? No, it defi-nitely is.

Way to screw things up, dude.

I briefly close my eyes, as her soft breathing sounds do little to relax me. We're obviously going to have to talk about this mistake, but I'm not so sure I should be here when she wakes up. That might just make things all that much more awkward. I inch away, and instantly miss her heat. Odd, considering I'm the guy who's quick to bail. I move around in the dark, and stub my toes on the corner of the bed.

Fuuuuuuck.

I hop around like a frog jacked up on Red Bull and clench down on my jaw to stifle a barrage of curse words. She moans in her sleep and with my foot in my hand, I stop bouncing around. I stand perfectly still as I wait for her to settle. She finally goes quiet and I gather my clothes. I hurry into them and do one last check in the dark to see if I left any traces of our night behind, but can't make out a goddamn thing.

I open the door as quietly as possible, and it clicks shut behind me. Bending forward, I brace my hands on my knees, and suck in a few deep breaths. Voices sound in the distance, and I straighten to my full height. Since I'm completely worked up, I can't imagine I'll get any sleep tonight.

I head down to the casino and grab a drink at the bar. A cute blonde settles herself on the stool beside me.

"Hi Cason."

"Hey," I say, and swirl the whiskey in my cup.

"I'm such a huge fan."

I cast her a smile. "Nice, thanks," I say and take a big drink of my whiskey. I welcome the burn down my throat, as I think about the mess I've gotten myself into.

"Would you mind autographing something for me?"

Any other time, I might have considered taking the blonde to bed, but now, I'm too fucked over and need to get my head on straight before I make any more mistakes tonight.

"Yeah, sure," I say and hold my hand out for a pen. She puts a marker in my hand, and opens her blouse to reveal breasts barely contained in a tiny lace bra. "Ah, yeah, okay." I scribble my name across her breasts when I spot Liam coming our way. He's not steady on his feet, and I'm guessing he lost his chance with Emily every bit as much as I had.

Oh, but you won something so much better.

He slaps me on the back. "Hey bud," he says.

"Liam, this is..." I pause and wait for the girl to give me her name.

"Lexi," she says.

"Liam, meet Lexi. What a cute couple you two make." I hand the marker to Liam, and slide from the stool, and Lexi jiggles her tits, looking for another signature.

I head back to my hotel room, and before I climb into bed, I put a call in for breakfast, for my room and Kinsley's. Tomorrow we'll have to talk—I think—and I don't want her hangry, plus I feel shitty for bailing. I snort. Like food is really going to make this all better.

I flop down onto my bed still dressed, and the next thing I know, there is a knock at my door. I blink my eyes open to discover it's not the middle of the night like I assumed. After that terrific round of sex, I'd obviously fallen into a deep sleep. Christ, my body hadn't been that worn out since our playoff games.

I push to my feet and rake my hand through my hair as I stumble toward the door. The fresh scent of coffee helps perk me up and I give the guy a big tip. I check my phone and groan. With so much going on, I'm not sure I'm going to have a chance to talk to Kinsley alone.

I take a big drink of coffee and jump in the shower. Twenty minutes later, after stuffing a few pancakes into my mouth, I go over the events of last night as I head downstairs to the lobby.

I spot Emily sitting in the lobby, and I stiffen as I get closer.

"Whoa, are you okay?" I ask as she sits there with her eyes closed.

She blinks one eye open, and groans. "Too much tequila," she says and taps the seat beside her. I sit down. "Uh, did I give you my room card last night?" she asks.

I nod. "Yeah, you did."

She groans louder. "I didn't mean to stand you up like that."

"It's not a problem." No, not a problem at all that I slept with a good friend, and ran out under the cover of darkness, leaving her to believe it might have been a dream. Yeah, not a problem at all.

I reach into my back pocket and pull out the key card. "Here," I say and she closes her hand over it.

"Keep it. I'll make up for it tonight."

I try to give it to her, but she's adamant that she doesn't want it back, but no way in hell can I sleep with her tonight after being with Kinsley. Hell it's not that I can't, it's that I don't want to.

I glance up to see Kinsley enter the lobby, dressed in a pair of cute jean shorts with frilled edges and a flowery blouse that showcases lush breasts my tongue had the pleasure of licking. My dick instantly hardens as her gaze flies to mine. Her eyes slowly drop to take in the push and pull between us with the room card, which looks like I'm trying to get it back from Emily's hands, when it's not like that at all. Kinsley's eyes widen, and she blinks rapidly. She steps closer and plasters on a smile. That's when I notice the love marks on her neck. Fuck. Her hand goes to said love marks, and she turns her focus to Emily when Emily asks a question.

"Kinsley, what happened to you last night?"

Kinsley takes a fast breath, her gaze sliding to mine. With confusion written all over her face, like she's still trying to figure out if last night was real or not, she looks at my neck, and earlobe—a very teeth lanced earlobe. A strange sound crawls out of her throat.

Guess she figured it out.

"Remember I said I had to go to my room last night," Emily says with an unlady like snort.

Kinsley turns from me and hugs herself. I take note of her quivering hands. "Yeah, but you couldn't remember why," she says, her voice as shaky as her fingers.

"Well I remembered why. I was going to get lucky." She laughs and jerks her thumb my way. "I gave Cason my key card."

"Oh, God," Kinsley croaks out as she stumbles backward.

Emily laughs. "You must have been sorely disappointed when you crawled into my bed and found it empty." Emily winks at me. "But like I said, I'll make up for that tonight." She closes her hand over mine, securing the key card in my palm.

"You thought..." Kinsley begins, her gaze bobbing back between the two of us. "Holy," she gasps as the tumblers fall into place. She backs up, hits a potted plant and when they both nearly topple I jump up and slide my arm around her.

"You okay?" I steady her body by anchoring it to mine, and even though it's not the time to be taking pleasure in her soft curves, my goddamn dick has a mind of its own. I mentally scold myself and pray she can't feel the thickness between my legs as I consider scooping her up and going for round two.

"I...uh...I don't know." Dark lashes flash rapidly over blue eyes. "I'm not sure of...anything."

"Emily, can you get Kinsley a cup of coffee please," I say, my reasons two-fold. One, she looks like she needs a strong cup of java to help clear her head, and two I need a minute alone with her.

Emily groans and pushes to her feet as I keep my arm around Kinsley and set her on the bench.

She swallows. "Last night..." she begins and stops. Wide worried eyes search my face, but she already knows the answer to the question lingering on her tongue.

"Yeah. It was me," I say. "I was there with you. You weren't dreaming."

She exhales sharply and leans forward clutching her stomach like she's in physical pain. "I didn't...I thought... dream. Ohmigod, I can't believe this."

"Do you dream about me, Kins?" I ask in a soft, sincere voice, somehow liking that crazy idea.

"Yes...no...I don't know. I just didn't think..." She goes so still, I'm not even sure she's breathing. "Ohmigod," she says again, her body shaking.

I put my arm around her, and pull her to me. "Hey, come on. It wasn't so bad was it."

"Bad?" She shakes her head. "I have never been more embarrassed in my life."

"What's to be embarrassed about? We're two consenting adults, and the sex was great."

"You thought it was great?" she asks, her big blue eyes wide.

"Yeah, it was fucking great. Didn't you think it was?" I know I'm not great at expressing myself with words, so I really hope this isn't coming out the wrong way, and making her feel worse.

"I..."

"Tell me the truth, Kins. You can be honest with me. We're friends."

"Friends who just slept together." She bends forward and groans again. "Ohmigod, so bad."

I nudge her playfully. "I believe it's called friends with benefits." She shakes her head and I ask, "Wait, are you saying the sex was bad for you?"

"My God, Cason, it was the best sex I ever had," she blurts out, then looks mortified when an elderly lady walking by stops, gasps, and gives her a mortified look. Kinsley puts her hand over her mouth. "Oops."

"Nothing to see here," I say. The white-haired lady with the small poodle tucked in her bag huffs and saunters off. "Okay, so it was the best sex. Not a problem then, right?"

"I figured it was so good because I was dreaming." She covers her face and peers at me through spread fingers. "I never knew it could be that good, to be honest. You did all the right things, but..."

I puff up my chest, loving that I satisfied her. "But what?"

"But," she says and inches away from me. "You thought you were crawling in bed with Emily."

"Ah, about that—" I begin and stop, because it's true. I can't dispute the fact that I thought I was crawling in bed with Emily. But once I found out it was Kinsley, it changed everything. The second our lips touch, I realized I was in the wrong bed, with the right woman. She's not the kind of girl I usually go for. That doesn't change the fact that we were explosive together, and when it comes right down to it...I want it again. Jesus, I'm such a typical guy, it's ridiculous.

"You...Emily..."

"Did someone just say my name?" Emily asks as she comes back with coffee in a paper cup, one for her, and one for Kinsley. How nice of her to think I might want one.

"Just wondering what was taking you so long," I say.

She huffs at me as she hands the cup over to Kinsley. "Ah, tequila. Hangover."

"Thanks," Kinsley says and takes a big sip of coffee.

Emily stands over her friend, her head cocked. "Kins, are you okay?" she asks, and tugs an elastic off her arm to tie her hair back. "You look like you could use a drink or ten, and it's not even noon."

"Yeah, just didn't get much sleep last night," she says and casts me a fast glance. "Strange bed. I would have slept in, but we all have a full list of wedding events planned for the day."

The elevator doors ping open, and out comes Rider and Jules followed by the other wedding guests. Liam saunters over to me, a shit-eating grin on his face.

"Had fun with Lexi, did you?" I ask.

"You missed out, bro. She was wild." He leans into me and says, "Wait, you don't look like you've missed out at all."

"What makes you say that?" I ask and shift uncomfortably. I don't normally talk about my bedroom antics with my friends. I leave it to their own imagination, and I'm sure most times it's better than the truth. Except for last night. Yeah, my teammates could never envision how great it was between Kins and me.

Liam laughs. "I guess you haven't seen all the bite marks, my friend." He lets loose a whistle. "It must have been one hell of a night."

I slowly turn my head, and find Kinsley staring at me wide-eyed. "Yeah, it was something."

"Who was she?" Liam asks. "I kind of like biters."

I take in a well-sated Kinsley, and a ridiculous stupid idea I have no right thinking races around my little pea-brain. The sex was great, we both agree to that, and we're adults doing what adults do. Maybe, if she wants, we could indulge in a little friends with benefits action while we're here for the wedding. What could it possibly hurt, as long as we're on the same page and agree to no regrets when it's over?

"Who she was is none of your business, and if she's going to bite anyone again, it's going to be me. No regrets. No expectations." Her eyes grow wide as she stares at me. "If that's what she wants."

KINSLEY

I f that's what she wants.

Of course, that's what she wants! Like he even has to ask.

"Cason, what are you saying," I mumble under my breath, not wanting anyone to hear. I know what he's saying, of course, but I guess I need him to straight up tell me he wants us to sleep together, using short sentences and small words, because I can't quite wrap my brain around any of this.

He gives a casual shrug. "You don't have to answer. Just think about it."

Okay, not the answer I was expecting but I don't press when conversation around us shifts to all the fun activities we'll be doing today. Too bad climbing the tallest observation tower in the USA, and hovering over the strip in a hot air balloon aren't on my list of awesome things to do. I'm freaking terrified of heights.

Cason shifts a bit closer, and his thigh touches mine, eliciting sparks in my body, mainly around my nether region. My tongue practically rolls from my mouth cartoon style and my clit quivers. Weird, right? Here I thought that was just something people say, something a person reads about in a book, but the macarena going on between my legs proves otherwise. There's definitely a party going on downstairs.

I had sex with Cason Callaghan.

Ohmigod, I had sex with Cason Callaghan!

But not just any run of the mill sex. No, of course not. He might be known as the Troublemaker, but he had no trouble finding and stimulating all the needy little spots on my body and leaving me blissfully sexed and sated, but at the same time...craving more.

My ex could never find any of my erogenous zones, even with the use of a guided map and instructions from me. I think he might have even asked Siri once. I naturally assumed last night's sex was good because it was a dream—everything my fantasies are made of—but this guy was better than any dream I've ever had.

Is he really suggesting we do it again?

Yeah, he is. I might not be his type, and this isn't about happily-ever-after or getting into a relationship, but a little fling while we're here? Now that sounds like a most awesome idea. He's right, we're consenting adults—friends. What could possibly go wrong?

A tortured needy sound I have no control over crawls out of my throat, and I'm about to tell him I don't have to think about it. The answer is yes, times a million squared. Is that a thing? Math is not my forte. But before I can open my mouth, his best friend Cole and his wife Nina enter the lobby.

I let loose a little sigh as I watch them. Back in Seattle, they visit my food truck frequently, and I've always liked the two of them, not to mention the way they look at each other. After being married for a few years, they still act like they're on their honeymoon. I'm a bit envious really. Men don't look at me like that. Never have. Never will. Especially when I'm with my best friend Emily.

She's every guy's dream girl: tall, blonde, thin. Basically, she's the antithesis of me, but I don't care. I'm not looking for anything long-term. Not anymore. After my ex dumped me because I quit Harvard, because I wasn't living up to his expectations—he didn't like me for me—it totally turned me off relationships.

As the door hit my ass on the way out, he was kind enough to tell me how lucky I was to have him. Apparently, I wasn't special and it'd be a cold day in hell before any man brought me home to meet their mother. You know what's not special? A guy who wanted to marry me to get ahead in my father's firm. I was the lucky one who dodged a bullet if anyone asked me. Still, on some level his words stung like a thousand angry hornets, and the truth is, I'm not the kind of girl guys go for, or bring home.

If I were, it would make things easier. Marriage would certainly convince my father that I've settled down and was ready to properly handle my large trust fund. Yeah, it's true. Believe it or not, I'm a trust fund baby, left to me by my grandfather who I miss dearly, and the funds were supposed to be signed over when I turned twenty-five—when my life was in order. But my father is holding it, because I didn't complete my law degree. I just couldn't do it, though. I was accepted to Harvard law school, following in Mom, Dad, and my two older sisters' footsteps, but I was miserable with a capital M.

Law is not my passion.

Sitting behind a desk for sixteen hours a day is not my passion.

Going before a judge is definitely not my passion.

Cooking...now that's where it's at. That's where I'm happiest.

Knowing that, I quit Harvard, at the risk of giving every member of my family a heart attack. Up until then I'd been the good girl, the one to go along without complaining. One day I woke up and realized just how depressed I was with the direction of my life. We only get one shot at this, so I traded the pens, pencils, and briefcase in for a barely working food truck in need of repairs. While it's hard work, everything about it fills my soul with happiness.

My food is a huge success in the neighborhood, but with zero collateral, the banks turned down my loan application. Not only is the truck held together by duct tape and a prayer, I want to rent space to start a restaurant that isn't on wheels.

My trust fund is on hold until I can prove to my father that I'm a grown up making grown up decisions. In my father's eyes, I guess the pink hair, tattoos, and piercings shout rebellion, not stability. I just want to be myself though, live my life on my own terms, and I honestly do not want to take a single dime from him, but this restaurant is important to me, and not just because it's my dream.

I want to make a difference in our community by giving back and helping the folks who have less. My restaurant will be about using locally sourced ingredients, and making special meals to help the homeless. I do that with my truck now, we also have a pay-it-forward program and I've been serving up tacos to the homeless for the past few months. I'm definitely in my happy place.

Speaking of happy places. My gaze slides to Cason's and our eyes lock. He took me to a place last night that I never knew existed, and dammit, I want to go there again.

"Are we all ready?" Jules asks as she slides her arm into her fiancé's.

I groan and Cason angles his head, his eyes still latched on me. "You okay?"

"I don't like heights," I say as I stand.

"You don't have to go."

He hovers over me, all raw strength, muscle, and assurance. "Yeah, I do. Jules wants this, and we go way back. I'd do anything for her."

"I can understand that," he says. "Cole is my best friend, and I'd do anything for him. I even let him marry my sister," he says with a laugh.

I grin, imagining how that must have gone down. "Also, I promised myself I'd be open to new things when I was here."

His brow raises, and my cheeks heat, knowing exactly where his thoughts have gone. Hell, mine have, too. As everyone heads outdoors to climb into the party bus, Cason leans into me and puts his mouth near my ear. "You were pretty open to things last night."

"Cason," I say and elbow him. He lets loose a loud oomph. "I don't want the others to hear and get the wrong idea...or the right idea...or any idea."

The corners of his mouth turn up in a grin so naughty I almost turn into a puck bunny and hand over my panties. Oh, how I'm going to do that later.

"I can be your dirty little secret if that's what you want," he murmurs.

"I—"

"Come on you two," Lindsay, Jules's best friend says. "You don't want us to leave without you."

"Oh yes, I do," I say under my breath and Cason gives my hands a squeeze.

"You got this. It'll be fun."

While I like his faith in me, I'm not sure I've got anything. I've been under such a tremendous amount of stress trying to keep my food truck in one piece, and doing a financial business plan for my restaurant, I've forgotten what fun was. I told myself I was going to forget about real life for the weekend, and just let go.

Thirty minutes later, after a champagne filled bus ride, I'm standing inside the observation deck, a floor to ceiling sheet of glass separating me from the outside deck. Many members of the wedding party chose to do one of the rides but the thoughts of catapulting over the edge of the tower to dangle weightlessly in the air—no thank you.

"You didn't have to stay with me. I'm a big girl," I say to Cason as he comes up behind me. He's so close I can smell his scent. It washes over me, and every inch of my body, from the top of my head to the tips of my toes, tingle in awareness. I hug myself to stave off a full body quiver.

"Maybe I wanted to stay behind." I'm about to protest when he says, "Let's go stand outside."

My legs quiver a bit harder. "I'm not sure I can do that."

"I actually think you'll like it if you give it a try."

"I'm not sure about that."

"Okay, how about this. If you hate it, tonight I'm all yours in bed, and if you like it, you're all mine, to do with as I like. What do you say?" he asks, that grin on his face so damn cute it's hard not to go up on my toes and kiss it off.

While those are two very hard choices, and I wouldn't complain either way, I say, "I never gave you my answer." I kind of like that he doesn't think I'm a sure thing—even though I totally am. I'd have to be the village idiot to turn down that offer.

"Yeah, I know, and I don't want your answer until the end of the day actually."

"Why is that?"

"Because I'm going to do everything in my power to convince you it's a good idea." He puts his hand on the small of my back and stretches out his fingers, until they're stroking the swell of my ass. He does not play fair.

"You're trouble, Cason," I say, interested to see how he plans to seduce me back into his bed, or my bed. Actually, it was Emily's bed, and that reminder momentarily fills me with unease. I shut it down quickly. He might have gone to her bed, but Cason is here with me now, because last night was fun.

He takes my hand and gives a gentle tug, leading me outside. A rush of air whips my hair from my shoulders, and sensations clutch my throat as he slowly walks me to the edge.

"I've got you. This is safe," he says as every muscle in my body squeezes tight. "Kinsley," he says so sharply my head jerks up and my gaze shoots to his.

"What?"

"For God's sake, breathe," he says laughing, and tension eases from my body as I take in a big breath of fresh—or rather polluted—air. Still, it helps relax me, and I get to lean on Cason, and that's not so bad either.

"I'm breathing, I'm breathing," I say, and put my arms around him, under the guise of being frightened, which I am, but this has more to do with copping a feel of his deliciously hard body.

"Want to walk around it, it's a great view of Vegas."

"Yeah, okay. Just don't let me go."

"I won't."

His arm wraps around me, and I absorb his strength and comfort, as we walk and he begins to point out landmarks. After a while, I relax even more.

"It is kind of cool up here," I say as I snuggle into Cason and take in the sights.

He wags his eyebrows playfully. "You know what that means."

"No, what?" I ask.

He stops walking, and turns into me, his hands on my shoulders. He casts a glance around, to make sure no one is paying attention to us, I assume, and then says, "You're having a good time, Kins. That means, you're mine tonight. Anything I want."

Oh, God, that sounds so awesome. I lift my chin an inch, bringing my lips closer to his. "But I still haven't said yes yet."

His grin is cheeky, and playful. "Not with words, but from the way you've been looking at me, and copping all the feels, your body is telling a whole different story.'"

"I am not copping all the feels." He arches a challenging brow. "Okay, much," I say and burst out laughing with him. His eyes narrow in on me, and he touches my chin, angles my mouth, and before I even realize what's going on, he's kissing me one-thousand feet above the ground. Technically it's not that high, it just feels it. But his kisses are leaving me breathless, like I am soaring into outer space. I moan into his mouth and his tongue plays with mine. Warmth bombards me, the pulse at the base of my neck climbing, and for the briefest of seconds, my stupid heart tries to get involved. But I am not allowing that. No way am I going to ruin our friendship by thinking this could be more. He's a known player, and I am not looking for any kind of relationship when I have a business that needs all my attention. Plus, guys suck.

Oh, how you loved when Cason sucked.

He breaks away and steals another glance around. "Shit, sorry. I shouldn't have done that. Not if you want to keep this a secret."

"We should don't you think?" I don't know why I'm asking that. Do I really want, or expect, him to say he wants to tell everyone what we're doing—because this might be more?

"Yeah, I do," he says and air leaves my lung in a hiss, leaving me feeling like a deflated balloon. Which is ridiculous! I don't want to start anything with him, and he clearly doesn't want to start anything with me. This is a brief Vegas affair...and what happens in Vegas. Well we all know the answer to that.

"Want to look through the viewfinder," I say, a little upset that my thoughts went down a road they had no right going.

"Sure."

We step up to the viewfinder, and I look through. It's hard to concentrate on anything though, especially with Cason standing so close behind me, his pelvis area nearly pressed against my backside.

"You go," I say.

"Nah, I've already seen it," he says. He throws his arm around me. "Besides I like the view up here on the deck better."

As his gaze moves over my face, I laugh. "How many times has that line worked for you?" I ask, even though I am a sure thing.

"Once?" he questions, an adorable grin on his face.

"No."

"Damn, I guess I'm going to have to pull out the playbook this time, huh?"

"You better bring your A-game if you want me in your bed tonight, pal," I say.

His cocky grin is back. "Are you sure you can handle my A-game, Kins?"

Lord, if he was playing with B-effort, then his A-game might just do me in—physically and emotionally. But I'm not about to tell him that. I want this.

I want him.

"I guess we're going to find out," I say.

5

CASON

I like her. A lot. I always have actually. She's funny and sexy and I love that she came here with an open mind. I never stopped to think about how hard she works, or how many hours she spends on her truck, but she's always behind the window cooking and serving up food. If I can help her have fun while here, then I'm all about it. When we return back home, things go back to the way they were. Kinsley doesn't want more than this, and I'm okay with that.

As the ropes holding the hot air balloon to the ground are released, and we begin to climb, she sinks to the floor. I squat with her. "Maybe a drink will help," I say and lift one of the bottles of champagne provided. The others are all looking over the edge, but Kinsley is looking a little pale.

"Liquid courage. I think that's exactly what's needed," she says. I grin, pop the cork and give her a generous amount. She sips it, and when it's gone, she holds her glass out for another. "You don't have to be down here with me," she says.

"I know, but I'm trying to seduce you into my bed, and I'm not going to win points if I just let you sit here in fear." That's not the entire truth. I am worried about her, and want to make this easier for her, but sometimes the words just don't come out right.

She chuckles. "Right, forgot about that." She takes another big drink.

"Want to get up?"

A big breath fills her lungs, and she lets it out slowly and nods. I stand and hold my hand out to her.

"Thanks," she says as I lift her and tug her into my side, securing her to me and hopefully giving her a sense of security. She wobbles a little. "This is insane," she says, and glances up into the balloon.

"But fun."

"Not yet," she says, and I laugh.

Emily shifts closer to us. "How you doing, Kins?" she asks, her gaze going back and forth between the two of us as I hold her. I think she's starting to get the idea that Kinsley is the biter Liam was talking about.

"I'm good," Kinsley says and grips the woven wicker edge.

"You have a mark on your neck," Emily says, and brushes Kinsley's hair from her shoulder.

"Curling iron," she says quickly. "I was super tired this morning when getting ready."

"You might want to put something on that," she suggests, and I bite back a grin, because yeah, I plan to put something on that again tonight—my mouth.

"I will, thanks."

Another bottle of champagne is popped and glasses are handed around. Kane holds his glass up and we all do the same. "To the couple who are tying the knot in..." He checks his watch. "Oh wow, less than five hours."

We all drink to that and Jules throws her arms around Rider and hugs him. The public display of affection is sweet —like a toothache. I groan. But seriously I'm so happy for them.

"What's the matter buddy?" Rider asks me. He obviously heard me groan.

I lift my glass and take a sip. "Nothing, I'm happy for you guys."

Cole pats me on the back. "Your turn is coming, my friend. Just wait and see."

"Nope, not happening," I say.

"Well I hope I catch the bouquet," Lindsay, Jules's best friend says, and smirks at Kane. They've been together for a long time now and that guy had better make his move soon. She's a great catch.

"Wouldn't it be funny if Kinsley caught it," Emily pipes in giggling.

Kinsley stiffens beside me.

"Why do you say that?" I ask.

Emily giggles some more, the champagne obviously getting to her. "After what her ex did, she's anti-marriage."

Kinsley chuckles uneasily, and I sense it's not something she wants every member of this wedding party to know. Jules reaches out and puts her hand on Kinsley's arm, giving it a little squeeze. "You can sit it out, Kins," Jules says, her eyes sympathetic. She obviously knows what happened between Kinsley and her ex. I remember when they broke up. It was right around the time she left Harvard and changed her outward appearance. The way she looks now much better suits her personality. But I didn't ask questions about her personal life or school. None of it was my business, and clearly something she wasn't interested in discussing.

"Come on, this is a party. So let's party," Kinsley says and takes another big drink. The mood switches back to a happy one.

"You okay?" I ask quietly as she turns to look out over the strip, her knuckles white on the hand gripping the basket.

"Embarrassed, maybe. I love Emily but sometimes she

says things before engaging her brain. She doesn't have a mean bone in her body, and didn't mean to embarrass me, but..."

"Your ex did a number on you, huh?"

She snorts, and shakes her head. "Let's just say I'm better off where I am."

"I agree," I say, and she smiles up at me, this time it reaches her eyes.

"You want me to take care of him for you," I joke, slamming my fist into my palm.

"It's okay. I'm so over him."

I go quiet for a moment. "I'm sorry he hurt you, Kins. I never really knew. If I'd known—"

"Would you have taken me out for ice cream?"

"Yeah, sure if that's something that would have made you feel better."

"Let's just say, last night was the only thing that has made me feel good in a long time."

"There's more where that came from," I tease, and move closer. Heat arcs between us and I glance around. Can the others feel this intense attraction growing between us? I hope not. My friends would be all over that, and Kins is a good friend. I'm not going to get involved any deeper, only for her to end up hurt because I can't seem to open myself up or say the right things.

"There's the Bellagio fountains," she says and points downward. "So pretty from up here."

"Then you are having fun," I tease.

"It's okay, I guess." She smirks at me, and maybe she doesn't want to admit it, maybe *she* wants to have her way with *me* tonight after the evening wedding ceremony.

Game on.

For the rest of the ride we all drink champagne, smack talk each other, and just relax and have fun. Most of the women are tipsy when we pile back into the party bus, and I make room for Kinsley to sit by me. She's smiling and happy, pushed through her fears, and ended up having a good time. I'm glad I could help with that. I spread my legs, until our thighs are touching and her little intake of breath doesn't go unnoticed. Her body is warm and soft next to mine, and my dick twitches, wanting a better viewing.

Liam stands on the seat and sticks his head through the moonroof and starts yelling at all the ladies walking down the street.

"Get back in here, you fool," Cole says. He tugs him in and jumps up himself to look out and we all laugh at his antics. Back at the hotel, everyone starts to go their own way to get ready for the ceremony.

I tug on Kinsley, keeping her back. "What room are you in?"

"Honeymoon suite," she tells me and I frown.

"You're kidding me."

"Nope, a screw up in my reservation and they bumped me up to high roller status," she says and pretends she's tossing the dice. "It's gorgeous, bigger than my condo."

"I'd like to see it."

She grins. "Is this your way of trying to get into my bed?"

"Well, yeah," I say and she laughs. I grip the hem of her T-shirt and bring her closer. "I'll come get you before the wedding."

"Like you're my date or something?"

"Or something," I say and when she wets those lush lips of hers, it's all I can do not to kiss the living fuck out of her. But I can't. Not here in the lobby, with far too many people watching. "Go," I say.

"What?" She blinks up at me, confusion in her big blue eyes.

"If you don't go right now, I'm going to ravage you."

She chuckles, but I get that she likes how crazy she makes me. Honest to God, I'm not sure what her ex did, or why they broke up, and it's his loss, but I'm glad I'm getting to spend this time with her.

"Aren't you forgetting something?" she asks.

"What?"

She reaches into her purse, and pulls out her extra key. "See you soon."

"Yeah, you will." She starts to walk away but turns back.

"Oh, and Cason. You still have Emily's key card. Try not to mix them up, unless..."

"Your room is the only one I want to go to, Kinsley," I say, my tone a bit harder to drive that point home.

She smiles. "I'll be waiting."

I take a few deep breaths and will my cock to settle as she saunters off toward the elevator. It's all I can do not to go after her but I have to get showered, shaved, and into my suit. As she stands at the elevator, I note the way some people stare at her. Why wouldn't they, she has bright pink hair and tattoos, but the truth is she's beautiful. She gives me a sexy little finger wave and climbs onto the elevator when the doors slide open.

"You doing her?" A voice asks from behind.

Shit.

I spin and find Liam standing there, a shit-eating-grin on his face.

"No," I say, a little put off by his choice of words. Technically I *am* doing her, but it's not like that between us. Well it is like that between us, it's just...

Fuck, I don't know what it is. All I know is I have a hell of a lot of respect for Kinsley and I don't want anyone dissing her.

"Yeah, right."

"You've got something to say, Liam?"

"Just that you might want to roll your tongue back into your mouth before you trip on it."

I exhale slowly, giving up the ruse. I know I promised to keep it a secret and I don't talk bedroom with the guys, except maybe Cole, but for some unknown reason, I want to talk about Kinsley, I want her name on my lips and that's a little messed up.

"Fine, I slept with Kinsley but keep it quiet okay. It was a mistake." Shit, wait maybe that was the wrong word to use.

"A mistake? You slip on a banana peel and fall in?"

"No, and never mind. Just keep this to yourself okay."

We head toward the elevator, and many heads turn our way. Lots of whispers and finger pointing, as people recognize us.

"You're saying Emily's fair game?" he asks, as he raises his hand and waves to some teenage boy staring wide-eyed.

"I never had any claims to Emily."

"Fine. I kind of like her."

"Of course, you do. What's not to like?" I ask.

"Exactly, my man," he says as we climb onto the elevator, people piling in behind us.

What's not to like?

Well, she doesn't have pink hair, tattoos, or piercings. She doesn't work her ass off running her own business, showing up seven days a week. She doesn't put her fears aside and climb the highest tower and float over the city to make sure her friend is having her best wedding experience.

Basically, she's not Kinsley.

Well, hell.

I get off on my floor and head to my room. I tug off my clothes, shower, and shave, and thirty minutes later, I'm back on the elevator on the way to Kinsley's suite. Her keycard is in my back pocket, but I think it's best if I knock. For some strange reason a burst of nervousness wells up inside me, but

I can't make sense of it. One thing I do know is how anxious I am to see her, just to be around her again.

I rap on the door, and when it swings open and I spot Kinsley in her bridesmaid dress, the light blueberry fabric hugging her sweet curves to perfection, I nearly bite off my fucking tongue.

Well, hell is right.

6

KINSLEY

My heart flutters as I take in the tall, gorgeous man before me. Wow, he cleans up nice. I let my gaze drop from his freshly shaved face, to his broad shoulders, and down to his tie and dress pants, which hug him to perfection. My ovaries take that moment to quiver. This man is every woman's fantasy come to life, and tonight he's mine. How did I get so lucky?

"Like what you see," he says, and my eyes go to his. He leans against the doorjamb, that adorable grin on his face again.

"Yeah, I do," I say, and tilt my head in a cocky manner.

"Am I a big fat snack, Kins?" he teases

"That and more," I admit.

"Still off snacking?"

I wave a dismissive hand and joke, "Diets are so yesterday."

"You want a piece of me?"

"No," I say, and he stiffens at that quick change in attitude. I grin at the worry in his eyes, and address it by adding, "I want all of you."

He relaxes. "I like a girl who knows what she wants. It's hot."

His eyes travel the length of me, a slow, leisurely inspection that leaves me quivering from head to toe.

"Like what you see?" I ask.

"Yeah, I do." One arm snakes out and he drags me to him. He cups my face. "Mind if I mess up this lipstick?"

"I can reapply," I say, and a second later his mouth is all over mine, kissing with a hunger and passion that zings through my body and settles deep between my legs. I put my arms around him, and he backs me up, presses me against the wall. He bends his knees and the steel rod below his belt presses against my sex. I groan and move against him. The last time I dry humped a guy and nearly got off was...never.

I'm breathless when he breaks the kiss, and the tortured look on his face matches mine. "You look gorgeous and I'm going to have a hard-on all night thinking about taking this dress off you," he confesses.

"Yes, Cason."

"Yes?"

"Yes, I had fun in the stratosphere and the hot air balloon," I say, letting him know he can have his way with me tonight.

"Fuck me."

"That's the plan," I say, and grin as I wipe my fingers over his bottom lip to remove the lipstick. "These smudges might raise questions, though." I go to the nightstand, and grab my purse. He follows me in.

"Nice room," he says as he explores the large space.

"I told you," I say but then realize he's used to big fancy places. The guy owns a damn mansion. I hand him a tissue and as he wipes his mouth, I reapply the ruby red lipstick.

"Listen I need to tell you something." He rocks on his

feet like a kid who just got caught with his hand in the cookie jar.

My stomach tightens at the seriousness in his voice, and I recap the lipstick and drop it into my purse. "It's okay, Cason," I say and avert my gaze.

He takes a step toward me, his presence big and overwhelming, even in the huge honeymoon suite. "What's okay?"

"You've changed your mind," I say.

Cason closes the distance, and tugs me to him in a move that is becoming familiar. "Your ex did a number on you, Kins. I am not having second thoughts."

"You're not?"

"No. If you don't believe me, believe this," he says and pushes his pelvis against me.

"Right." My heart takes flight as his erection indents my stomach. Dammit, dammit, dammit. Why did my brain go straight for the worst? I guess that's what happens when your ex tells you you're not special, just before dumping you, and there is a part of you that believes he might be right. But Cason, he *does* make me feel special, and I shouldn't jump to the wrong conclusions. He deserves better than that from me.

"I wanted to tell you that Liam knows about us. I lied but the bastard could see right through me. I told him to keep it to himself, and I'm sure he will."

I shrug. "I guess that's okay. He's kind of wild and crazy but I think he's a good guy."

"He's interested in Emily, actually."

I laugh. "Who isn't?"

"Me." He brushes his thumb over my cheek and my knees weaken. God, when he looks at me like that...touching me with easy tenderness. It's almost impossible to keep my heart out of the scenario. I have to though. I am not going down that road again—it only ends in disaster.

I try to make light of it and say, "You know all the right things to say, don't you?" He inches back, his jaw tight as he scrubs his face. Ah, did I hit a sore spot? "Cason?"

"Actually, I never say the right things, not when it comes to the important stuff."

Did he just say none of this was important—that maybe I wasn't important? I try not to react like I've been slapped and quickly remind myself that we're just having fun together.

I steal a glance at my phone to check the time. "We should go."

He pinches the bridge of his nose. "Wait, I don't think that came out right, Kins."

"It's okay, Cason. I understand," I say, because I do. I get what this is, and what it isn't and I'm okay with that. "We better hurry, they're all probably holding the bus for us."

Five minutes later, we're downstairs being ushered onto the bus. Rider and Jules are in the limo in front of us. Energy and excitement fills the space between us as we head to the chapel, but my thoughts are on Cason, and the way he has casually thrown his arm over the seat and is lightly brushing his thumb over my neck. The soft caress stimulates every erogenous zone in my body, and I squeeze my thighs together.

I angle my head to see him, but he's in a conversation with Cole about some hockey play they did last season. I get the sense that he's fully aware of what he's doing to me though. I take in all the smiling faces, and grin when I see Emily and Liam laughing easily together. The bus stops in front of the chapel, and my breath catches when we enter.

"It's beautiful. Classy and elegant," I say, and Cason puts his mouth near my ear.

"You were expecting Elvis?"

I laugh. "No, but I...I guess I just didn't know what to expect. Although I have to say, my grandmother loves Elvis."

"You're smiling."

"I love my grandmother." I take a deep breath, and let it out slowly, as I think about Gram. "She's the only one who never gave me a hard time when I left school." He frowns at me, and needing to lighten things up I say, "My parents would be mortified if I ever had a Vegas Elvis wedding, but Gram," I stop and chuckle. "She'd love it."

"She sounds like she marches to the beat of her own drum." He nudges me lightly. "Like you."

"She's a character. I bet you'd love her."

"How could I not love her, when she's just like you?"

My smile falls. Wait, what did he just say?

"I mean...uh." He tugs on his hair, clearly reading the shock on my face. "I don't mean I love you. I mean like a friend, yeah." He shakes his head, and says. "Let me try this again. If I like you, I'd like her, and hey, maybe when you get married you can have it in Vegas. If it makes you and your grandmother happy who cares what anyone else thinks."

My heart squeezes. "I care, Cason."

He frowns like that takes him by surprise. "How come?"

I purse my lips and toy with the lace on my dress as I consider my answer. "I'm such a disappointment to my family. I was supposed to follow in their footsteps and when I quit they were all pretty upset with me, they still are, actually."

His head rears back like I just slapped him, which stops me from telling him about my trust fund. My God, I've already said too much as it is. We're friends, but he's not my confidant, and he doesn't need to know about my problems. We're here to have fun, and I am not going to drag him down.

"Kins, that's crazy. I—"

He doesn't get to finish when a middle-aged lady claps her hands, effectively cutting off whatever it was Cason was going to say.

"Let's all get organized now," she says, directing Rider to

head to the altar. I turn to see Jules enter, and my throat squeezes tight as she stares at her soon-to-be husband, the two sending secret messages to one another.

I step up to Jules and give her a big hug. "You're beautiful." She squeezes me, and the music starts. I was originally paired up with Liam, the two of us were supposed to walk down the aisle first, but Cason bumps him out of the way.

"My guess is you want to pair up with Emily," he says, and Liam gives him a knowing smirk.

I make light and turn back to Jules. "They're kind of hooking up. Do you mind if I walk with Cason?"

"Actually, I think that's a much better pairing," she says with a grin. Jules never did like my ex, and after we broke up, she was constantly trying to set me up, but I had no time or inclination to date.

"It's not like that," I say, and her grin widens.

"Oh, but it's still early. Plenty of time for it to be like that."

I roll my eyes, and slide my arm into Cason's. As we head toward the altar, the scent of his freshly showered skin reaches my nostrils. I inhale to fill my lungs, and the strangest image of Cason standing up there waiting for me, races through me. Wow, where the heck did that come from? Must be all the pumped oxygen in this place. It's messing with my brain.

We part when we reach the front and turn to watch the others make their way. Emily and Liam come, followed by the others until Jules is standing there with Kane, who's giving her away. Jules and Rider both come from big families and instead of everyone flying here, they opted to get married with friends and have a big party at home.

Tears fill my eyes as Kane walks her to her best friend and lover, and I have to say, I'm a little envious of them. I catch the way Cason is studying me, and I sniff back the tears, as the two exchange vows. My throat is raw, tight when the two of them leave the chapel married, and we follow them out.

"I need a drink," I mumble to myself.

"Good, because I need ten," Cason says.

"Really?"

"Weddings."

Wow, he really has something against weddings. That thought evaporates and a thrill goes down my spine as he steps closer to me. "Good thing it's an open bar, then," I tell him.

We all pile back into the bus and we're taken back to the hotel, to a private room with tables full of hor d'oeuvres. A server walks by with a tray of champagne, and Cason removes two glasses. He hands me one, we clink, and he drains his glass.

"You know what that tastes like?" he asks.

"No, what?"

"Another."

I grin and take another sip.

"Actually," he says. "Let's go for the hard stuff."

"Hard stuff, huh?" I joke and shift my body so I can lightly run my hand over his cock without anyone seeing. He jumps beneath my touch.

"Jesus, woman. Is that all you think about?" he scolds, even though he's pushing against my palm and growing thicker by the second.

I laugh. "When I'm with you, yeah, and you're one to talk."

He puts his hand on the small of my back. "Come on." He walks me to the bar, and orders shots of tequila.

"Are you trying to get me drunk?" I ask.

"No, I'm trying to get me drunk," he says, and for a brief second I spot something in his eyes. Something sad and dejected, something that wraps around my heart and squeezes tight. What is going on with him? He's usually light and playful but I'm suddenly sensing something deep and serious. What kind of demons does this man have?

"So you've never thought about marriage?" I ask.

"Nope," he says quickly, so quickly I can't help but think he's not being truthful, with me or himself.

"What do you have against marriage?"

Instead of answering, he holds his fingers up, gesturing for two more tequila. They come and he hands me one.

"Were you hurt?" I push, wanting to know what makes this man tick.

"Let's just say I don't have what it takes to do long-term, Kins. I'm pretty much a two-week kind of guy."

"You bail after two weeks?"

"Something like that." This man has so much to offer. What the hell is he afraid of? He doesn't seem commitment phobic to me, but if he's telling me he bores after two weeks, who am I to say otherwise? I'm about to ask why, what it is about long-term that frightens him, but he takes a big drink and gestures to the dance floor.

"Dance with me," he says and I close my mouth. If he's redirecting the conversation by dancing, it's definitely a conversation he doesn't want to have.

We hit the dance floor, joining our friends, and soon enough the hours disappear, so does the tequila. By the time Jules is ready to toss the bouquet, I'm so buzzed and having so much fun, I'm game.

I muscle my way through the girls, and they all laugh and throw their arms around me. Jules looks over her shoulder, and grins when she sees me. She tosses the flowers and if a scout from the NBA was here, I'd be their first draft pick, because let me tell you, forget energy drinks, tequila's what really makes you fly. I jump high and snatch the bouquet right out of the air and everyone laughs and claps when I land and take a bow.

"And here you said you were afraid of heights," Cason says when I saunter over to him, all proud of myself.

"I got air, huh?" I ask, smelling the flowers. The room spins a little around me.

"Want to get some air, for real," Cason says. "Jules and Rider are leaving, and it looks like everything is settling down."

"Fresh air, yes, please," I say and he puts his hand on my back to lead me out to the strip. The heat of his palm seeps under my dress and curls around me. I shiver.

"You cold?" he asks.

"Hot," I say.

"Yeah, you are," he says and nibbles his bottom lip.

"I think we might have had too much tequila."

"It's possible," he says with a laugh.

Cheers break out down the block and I snatch his hand. "Let's go see what's going on."

We practically skip down the strip, dodging pedestrians. Our feet come to an abrupt halt when we spot Elvis. "What's going on?"

A girl leans into me, and says, "Impromptu marriages. I don't think they're real though. Just for fun." She looks at my flowers. "Is that a bridal bouquet?"

"Yup."

She lifts her hand. "Over here," she says, getting Elvis's attention.

"I do have the honeymoon suite," I say to Cason.

He arches a brow, and he's so damn hot, I could melt at his feet. "Think we should put it to use?"

CASON

I roll over and peel my tongue from the roof of my mouth. Jesus, how many shots did I have last night anyway? Kinsley moans in protest as the bed dips and I climb from the sheets, tuck her in and make my way to the bathroom.

I take one look at my sorry self in the mirror and if I had pants on, I'd have jumped straight out of them. I wonder if Kins got the license plate of the truck that ran me over. Probably dinged her, too. We both work super hard at our jobs, and I haven't really drank in a long time—neither of us has. I guess we both made up for that last night.

Brain still foggy, I brush my teeth, rinse with mouthwash, and climb into the shower. The hot water is glorious against my aching body and deep between my legs my cock twitches, a reminder of all the sex Kinsley and I had last night after getting...married?

Wait, what?

Right, right, we went through with that fake ceremony as a joke. I reach for the shampoo and that's when I notice my college ring is missing from my finger. Shit, did I lose it? I pour a generous amount of shampoo into my palm and soap up. As I wrack my brain to retrace my steps from last night, the fog finally clears and I grin. I gave Kinsley the ring last night. Put it on her finger during the ceremony. It was kind of big for her, so I hope it hasn't slipped off.

A noise behind me gains my attention, and I turn to see Kinsley brushing her teeth. My dick instantly hardens, despite the sex-a-thon last night.

"Want to join me?" I ask.

"Yeah, right after I take something for this headache." She reaches into her cosmetic bag, pulls out some pills, and swallows them. "You?" she asks.

"No, I'm good. The shower helps."

She comes toward me, reaches her hand up to her face, and goes perfectly still when she finds my ring on her index finger. "Wait, why do I have this?" she asks. I give her a minute and she smiles. "Oh, right." She steps into the shower. "Move over fake husband," she says. "You're hogging all the hot water."

"Nagging wife already." I chuckle softly, not wanting to jolt her headache. "I thought the honeymoon stage would be longer."

"It's your fault I feel like someone drove over me with my food truck."

I tug her to me. "Poor baby. I bet I can make you forget all about that headache."

With her back to my chest, she lays her head against my shoulder and excels a soft sigh as I cup her breasts and rub them gently. Her nipples pucker under my touch and Jesus, I love how responsive she is, always so open and eager.

"That's so nice, Cason," she murmurs.

I stroke her lightly. "Headache easing?" I ask as I slide one hand lower to part her damp lips.

"Yeah..." she says.

"Are you too sore for me?"

"Probably," she says, "But that doesn't mean I don't want you again."

"I want you, too," I say, and she wiggles against my thick cock.

"I can tell."

"Today is our last full day in Vegas," I say, and I'm not sure why I'm reminding her of that. Is it because I want her to know when we leave, it's over, or is it because I want her to tell me that it doesn't have to be over?

Shit, I can't go there with her. She's my good friend, and I don't want to hurt her, the way I always seem to hurt every woman I'm with. I'm emotionally closed off, can never say the right thing at the right time. Kins is the last woman I ever want to hurt.

"Yeah, life goes back to normal," she says, reminding me she's sticking to the timeline we set out, which is a good thing. Then why do I feel like I've been hit in the gut with a runaway puck? "Well, sort of normal."

I lightly stroke her clit and she moans. "What does sort of normal mean?"

I run my hand over her wet pussy, petting her softly, soothing the soreness of last night and she relaxes even more in my arms.

"I'm looking to open a restaurant. It's my dream, actually."

"That's great, Kins. I never knew that."

"Yeah," she says but it holds a measure of sadness.

I put both hands on her shoulder and turn her until she's facing me. There is so much uncertainty in her eyes, it momentarily catches me off guard. "What?" I ask.

"Nothing," she says, brushing off my question as her hands go to my chest for a slow exploration. She touches me lightly, tracing my nipple before moving on to the grooves in my stomach.

"I love your abs," she murmurs.

I laugh. "Good, now tell me what's wrong."

She shrugs. "It's just...I can't get a loan, and my trust fund is being held captive by my father."

"You have a trust fund?"

She cringes like that makes her a bad person. "Yeah. Left to me by my grandfather. That sounds awful doesn't it?"

"Kinsley, there's nothing wrong with a trust fund. I set one up for my sister ages ago. Sometimes we need a little help."

"The thing is though, Cason, I didn't follow in my family's footsteps, and they sort of disowned me. Everyone except my grandmother."

Anger rips through me, and my body tightens. "That's pretty fucking shitty."

Her head jerks up at the harshness in my words.

"You think so?"

"Yeah, I think so. You're their goddamn daughter. They should be happy for you. Cooking is your passion. Anyone can see that. Why would they want you to spend the rest of your life doing something you don't want to do? You only get one shot at this life, you know. You should be doing what makes you happy."

She smiles at me, so bright and startling, so full of gratitude, it seeps under my skin, and my throat tightens.

"Funny, that's what I said to myself. Those exact words were the reason I quit school and bought an old truck."

I touch her face, lightly brush my thumb over her flushed cheek. "Beautiful and smart."

She puts her head on my chest, and goes quiet for a moment. I grab the soap and start washing her up. "I really like that you see this my way. No one else seems to."

"So, what's going on with your trust fund?"

"I wish I could do what I want without it, but with no collateral or co-signer, and a truck that is rolling on four tires because I shoot up a prayer every night, I can't get a loan. My father won't sign my trust fund over until I can prove I'm stable and not going to blow it on piercings or tattoos. Crazy."

"It is crazy, and I happen to love your tattoos and piercings. They represent who you are, and you should always be true to yourself, Kins."

"You always say the right things," she says, and my heart misses a beat.

A half-laugh half-snort crawls out of my throat. "You're the only one who's ever said that to me. Normally, I say all the wrong things."

"Maybe it's because we're friends," she says. "We both know what's going on here isn't about more."

My stomach drops at the reminder. Why? Oh, maybe some part of me wants to try to work things out with Kinsley. We're good now, but if we delved into a deeper relationship would I be able to give her what she wanted, say the things she needed to hear?

"Yeah, maybe. What do you need to do to prove you're stable?"

She laughs. "Oh, I don't know, remove my piercings, cover my tattoos, dye my hair back. Get married and stay married for at least thirty days."

I nod at that. "Too bad last night's ceremony was fake. That would have helped you out quite a bit." I move her around, until the hot spray washes the soap from her body.

"Well it was, and marriage is definitely not in my future, so I have to figure out some other way." Once we're both rinsed off, I grab a big fluffy towel and wrap her in it. I scoop her up and she yelps in surprise.

"Ohmigod, remember last night when you carried me through the door and over threshold of the room, because we were married and about to consummate."

"Vaguely," I say, and she laughs.

"That was fun."

"That's what Vegas is all about."

She frowns. "We're supposed to meet the others for brunch and a tour of Red Rock Canyon."

"Yeah," I say. "I wish we didn't have to go."

"Really?" Kinsley says. "I don't want to go either. Do you think they'd be upset if we blew them off?"

"Probably not," I say. "They did see us putting back the tequila."

"I was thinking then, maybe we can stay in this bed. The only thing I want to blow off is you," she says and takes my cock into her small hand. She gives me a light squeeze and I groan, loudly. "I'll text Jules," she says. "I have a feeling she thinks there is something going on between us anyway, and since she's been trying to set me up for ages, she'll be happy to think we're spending the day in bed."

I set her down and her towel falls from her gorgeous, lush body as she goes in search of her purse.

"I didn't realize she was trying to set you up."

"Probably because I refuse every time?"

"How come?" I ask and sit on the edge of the bed.

She looks at me over her shoulder. "You were right when you said my ex did a number on me."

"I'm sorry, Kins." She pulls out her phone and sits on the other side of the bed, across from me.

"I honestly dodged a bullet, Cason. He was an asshole and was only with me to get ahead in my father's firm."

"I'm going to find his sorry ass and beat it."

She laughs. "See, you do say all the right things, but no,

you are not going to do that. He's in the past, and I'm over him."

I eye her as she averts her gaze and slides her finger across the screen. "But..."

"Why is it I can't get anything by you?"

"You don't have to tell me if you don't want to, but like you said, we're friends, and if you want to talk, I'm here. You're over him, but you're not over something."

"You're right." She runs her fingers through her damp hair. "He told me I was nothing special. That I was chubby and lucky to have him. That I wasn't the kind of girl guys were attracted to, and no one would ever stay with me for any length of time."

"Motherfucker," I say and clench my fists. "I am going to kill him, Kinsley."

"No, you're not."

I frown at her as realization dawns. "Wait, you don't believe that, do you?"

"I don't know, Cason. I'm not—"

Before she can even get the words out, I'm on my feet, crossing to the other side of the bed. I kneel down in front of her. I might not always say the right things, but actions speak louder than words anyway. I lean in and press my lips to hers. My kisses are slow, leisurely, a gentle reintroduction to her body. How any man could call this woman chubby is beyond me. She's plump and curvy and goddammit, I want to sink my teeth into her again, to show her just how desirable and special she really is.

"Cason," she murmurs when my mouth leaves hers to travel to that sensitive spot on her neck. I pepper her with hot, wet, open mouthed kisses until she's moaning and chanting my name. Jesus, I love hearing it on her lips.

"So beautiful," I murmur and take one full breast into my mouth for a deep taste. Her hands go around my head, and she holds me to her, like she's afraid her ex was right and I might just flee.

I pay homage to one breast and then the other, as I widen her legs even more, making room for myself. My dick throbs, so eager to be inside her again, but he's going to have to wait. I need to worship every inch of her delectable body, and leave no doubt in her mind she's a sexy goddess and any man would be blessed to have her. Right now, I'm the luckiest goddamn man in the universe to be here with her like this.

Her nipple plops from my mouth, and her eyes are glazed over when I inch back to see her.

"Cason," she says.

"I'm here, Kins. I'm not going anywhere." I give her shoulders a little nudge and she falls backward on the bed, her legs dangling over the edge. I pick up her thighs and place them over my shoulders and she goes up on her elbows to watch.

"This pussy," I say as I part her damp folds. "The sweetest, sexiest pussy I've ever seen." Heat colors her neck and cheeks a sexy pink, and I lick at her, swirl my tongue through her hot arousal until she's writhing beneath me. "I want to spend the day right here, Kins. Right here with your sweet pussy, giving you orgasm after orgasm." She moans, and drops back onto the bed, her fingers fisting the sheets, as I eat at her like a man starved, and put a finger inside her. Unbelievable how much I want her, really, considering the amount of times I was inside her last night.

Her sex squeezes my finger, and I move it in and out, the way she likes. I lightly stroke her bundle of nerves inside, and press my lips to her clit. I drag my teeth over it, and her moans grow louder.

"Yeah, that's it," I say, wanting her to let go of past hurts and blossom beneath my touch. A girl like her needs to know her worth, needs to be with a man who can help her understand and appreciate her value. Just the way she is. She doesn't need to change a thing about herself, not for her family or for any man. Goddammit that pisses me off, but I'll give it more consideration later. Right now all I want to do is get lost in the taste of her as I bring her to climax.

I put another finger inside her and her muscles slowly start to spasm, but I don't want her to fall over the edge just yet. I am so not done with her. I finger fuck her a few more times, and she moves and shifts and bangs against my mouth. I love everything about this. I put my tongue high inside her and place my thumb over her clit. I circle it, and she growls with frustration. I chuckle at her neediness, and like how much she wants this from me.

"Need something, babe?" I ask.

"Yes, I need you," she says. It's not the answer I expected. Here I thought she'd say she needed to orgasm, but she said she needed me.

Don't read too much into that Cason.

"Tell me what you need," I say and run my tongue from the bottom of her hot pussy to where my thumb is applying a light amount of pressure.

"I need you inside me, Cason. I want your mouth on my body and your cock in my pussy," she says, and my heart thumps a little harder against my chest.

"I'll give you what you want, Kins."

"Yesss," she hisses and I switch things up again, putting my fingers back inside her and taking her clit into my mouth. I eat at her, and finger fuck her, until she's panting, and then I change the pressure and rhythm, until she's crying out my name, her head tossing back and forth. That first sweet clench around my fingers is pure bliss—for the both of us. I swear to God, it's as good for me as it is for her. Her hot cum drips down her thighs, and I put my mouth right there, to lap up every last delectable drop. She continues to spasm around my fingers, and I hold still inside her, to give her something to clench around.

Her spasm stops and she reaches for me, a desperation about her as she pulls me on top of her. "Cason, your cock, please."

My entire body is quaking as I nod, quickly slide on a condom and fall back over her. I kiss her deeply, my cock at her opening, but I want her differently this time. I want her to ride me.

I stand up, and take her with me. Her eyes are a bit confused, until I sit on the edge of the bed, with her on my lap.

"Oh, yes," she says.

I let her shimmy back a bit so she can rest her knees on the bed, and I lift her over my cock, which is poised and aimed as I bring her back down onto it. A gasp catches in her throat as I fill her completely, and lean in to lick her hard nipples as she rotates her hips and stimulates her core with every inch of my dick.

"So damn good," she murmurs, and I grab her hips to take control of the movement. I move her on my cock, lift her up and down and gyrate her body until I'm a fucking goner.

"Kins," I murmur and she bends forward to find my mouth. I piston into her faster. Hard blunt strokes that bring on her second orgasm. Her mouth opens, her eyes latched on mine, and we just stare at each other, open and honest as we give in to the pleasure tearing through our bodies.

"Fuck," I say as I climax high inside of her, for the first time in my life wishing there was no condom so I could feel skin on skin as her hot juices poured from her body.

Her breasts press against me as she puts her arms around my body to hold on tight. I pant and gasp and struggle for air with each spurt, and once I'm depleted and she stops clenching, I put my head on her shoulder and wrap my arms around her, squeezing her to me.

We stay like that for a long time, neither speaking, lost in our own thoughts as we regulate our breathing.

"We'll never be able to hide this from the others," she says, and I inch back to see the sated smile on her mouth.

"One look at us and they'll know we've been fucking all night."

"Yeah, then they'll all make a big deal out of it, when it's not a big deal at all," she says with a laugh.

Her words shouldn't sting, they shouldn't feel like a punch to the gut, but somehow they do. Wanting to keep things light, she obviously does, too, I move my hips, my near flaccid cock still inside her and say, "Well there was something big."

She laughs hard, like my joke has taken the weight of the world off her shoulder. "Okay, big. I'll give you that," she says and makes a move to climb off me. I grip her hips to help her, and she makes a trip to the bathroom as I dispose of the condom. My stomach takes that moment to growl. I tug on my boxer shorts, and reach for the phone to order us in some food.

She comes back into the room, her body warm and flush, and so inviting. Her purse catches her eyes, and she bends, presenting me with her ass. That's not a smart move on her part, unless she wants me to ravish her like that.

"What's this?" she says.

As I hit the button for room service, she pulls a sheet of paper from her purse and opens it. Her face pales slightly as she reads it and her eyes are as big as saucers when they meet mine. What the hell is on that paper that has her so spooked?

"Um, Cason. I think we have a problem. A big one."

8

KINSLEY

"**W**hat are you talking about?" he asks and I hand over the paper with shaky fingers.

"We, ah, kind of did a thing." A big thing. A horrible thing. A thing that we need to undo before anyone finds out. God, I was the one who suggested we put the honeymoon suite to good use, and this is the last thing he wants. Is he going to hate me? Will this come between our friendship?

He reads the marriage license, and while a part of me is praying it's not true, that it's just part of the ruse last night, there is another part that knows it's absolutely real. I might not be a lawyer, but I do know a legally binding contract when I see one—sober.

"No fucking way," he says and grips his hair and tugs. "This isn't real..." His eyes lift, lock on mine. "Is it?"

"I actually think it is," I say, and twist my fingers together, the knot in my stomach so tight, I can hardly breathe. "I'm so sorry."

"Holy fuck, Kins," he says with a snort. "People really do go wild in Vegas."

As my mind goes back to last night to piece things together, I realize I'm still naked. Feeling exposed in far too many ways, I grab a robe from the bathroom, slide it over my shoulders and sink down on the edge of the bed where Cason is still reading the paper. Maybe he thinks if he stares at it long enough, the words will change or it'll spontaneously combust. I don't have that kind of luck.

"It has our signatures," he says. "I didn't know your middle name was Elizabeth."

"Ohmigod, is that what you're taking from this?" I ask, my voice bordering on hysteria.

He frowns like he's in deep thought. "Wait, are you going to take Callaghan for your last name or keep Palmer? Or maybe you want to hyphenate. Although Kinsley Elizabeth Palmer Callaghan really is a mouthful."

Speaking of mouths, mine is practically on the floor. Why is he acting so cavalier? We just got married for God's sake. Why isn't he freaking out, too? "Cason," I say. "What are you doing?"

"I don't know. Sometimes I ramble and just say the wrong things. Especially when I'm a little thrown off." He shakes the paper. "Or a lot."

Ah, okay, now I'm getting a glimpse into the Cason who sometimes says the wrong things. "This is serious, Cason."

"Sorry. I'm just...hey, it's okay," he says when he sees my tightening shoulders. But it's not just my shoulders reacting negatively to this distressing news. My damn hands are shaking, and I'm on the brink of tears.

"Cason, if my family ever got wind of this, they'd never, ever forgive me, and my trust fund would instantly be absorbed into their estate." I stand and start to pace. "An impromptu wedding with a friend, after too much tequila, yeah, that just screams I'm adulting and nailing it."

He folds the paper and sets it on the nightstand. He goes

so quiet, and for a minute I think he might have fallen asleep while sitting up.

"We're really married, Kins," he finally says, his voice a low, soft whisper. "Consummated it, too, numerous times. I guess there is only one thing we can do now."

"Get it annulled," I say at the exact time he says, "Stay married for thirty days."

Wide-eyed, we both stare at each other, our addled brains working to process what the other just said.

"We can't do that," I say. "This isn't real. We're friends."

"Yeah, but look at it this way. I'm not interested in a long-term relationship with anyone, so it's not like this will be holding me back from finding someone I want to get serious with, and maybe for thirty days, we can pretend, and you can get your trust fund."

He stands and puts his hands on my arms. He gives a little squeeze, but I'm definitely not reassured. "No way, I could never ask you to do that. I won't."

"You didn't ask. I offered, and we're already married, Kins. All we'd have to do is pretend it's a real one."

"This is insane." I tug on my hair, and take deep gulping breaths. "We'd never be able to pull it off."

He shrugs. "With the right motivation, we can do anything."

"Motivation. What do you mean?"

He pulls me to him. "I get to have sex with you for another thirty days."

"Really? You want that?"

His grin is sexy and adorable when he says, "Yeah, I want that."

I nod in understanding. "You do seem to kind of enjoy it." He lets out a big laugh and it eases some of the tension coiled in my stomach.

"So do you," he says.

"True, but I don't know, Cason. You already told me you're a two-week kind of guy. If we go through with this, how can I expect you to last a whole month without getting bored?"

"I never said I leave because I get bored, Kinsley."

"Why do you leave?" I ask, really wanting to know. He looks like he's about to push away right now, but I hold him tight. "Hey, you're my husband now. I deserve to know the answer."

A pained look crosses his face. "Fine. It's not them, it's me, or rather it's them. No, it's me."

"Yeah, that clarifies everything."

He chuckles, but it holds no humor. "Kins. If you haven't noticed, I have a bit of a hard time expressing myself." He blows out a fast breath. "How personal do you want me to get here?"

I glance at the unmade bed. "I think we've been as personal as two people can be, Cason, and you were pretty good at expressing yourself then."

"Okay, my parents were pretty absent when I was growing up. I was never really shown affection, and I have a hard time showing it to others. I never seem to say the right things at the right times. I swear to God, I mess up every relationship I've ever been in and end up hurting the person I'm with. Now, I get out after two weeks, before deeper feelings evolve, and no one gets hurt."

I'm stunned at what he's telling me, and sense there is more. "Go on."

"I have this knack for fucking things up and for hurting others. I'm told I'm closed off inside, unable to give what's needed, and I don't disagree. Simple as that." His eyes search mine. "But this is fake, so to speak. You're anti-marriage, and neither of us is looking for more, so what can I possibly fuck up? We're not trying to build a relationship, and we're friends so it's not like one of us will fall in love and get hurt. Wait, I'm not even sure that came out right."

I let that circle my brain for a minute. Okay, so he's saying he's not going to fall in love with me, nor me him—oh, how little he knows—but if I keep my feelings to myself, and go along with this, it's the perfect way to get my hands on my trust fund. I can get the truck fixed up and finally open my restaurant. "Thirty days," I say quietly. "You really think you could pretend to be my husband for one full month?"

"Yeah, I do. Sex and all the tacos I can eat. I can handle that."

I arch my brow. "I don't remember anything about all the tacos you can eat."

"That a deal breaker, Kins?"

I laugh. "No, not really."

"I'm on break from hockey practice. Lots of time for us to spend together which will really help sell this marriage to your parents."

I cringe. "What about our friends? They'll know better."

"Yeah, you're right. I guess we'll tell them the truth." He rolls one shoulder. "We'll just let them know I'm just helping you out. They don't need to know anything else."

"That's probably for the best." I twist my lips. "What about your parents?"

"They don't need to know anything," he says. "We'll likely have an annulment before I even see them again, anyway."

"That makes sense." I glance down for a second. "Is it wrong that we're doing this?" My stomach takes that moment to ache. "I don't like deceiving anyone. I don't even really want to take the trust fund. God, I sound so privileged."

"I told you there is nothing wrong with a trust fund, Kins. You work harder than anyone I know. Your father is using it to control you."

"If I could find another way to get my business off the ground, I would."

"What does your grandmother say? I'm assuming your grandfather that left you the money was her husband, or am I wrong?"

"No, you're right, and she doesn't know. Not that I know anyway. I'm not about to bring it up and upset her."

"Your grandmother and grandfather would want you to have the money to use as you wish, I'm sure. I think grandma knows you well enough to know you wouldn't blow it, Kins."

I smile up at him, and say, "Just so you know, all-you-can-eat tacos will ruin that perfect six pack."

"You think I'm perfect," he jokes.

"Perfectly full of yourself, yes," I shoot back. I briefly close my eyes as he chuckles. "I still can't believe this happened."

"We just happened to be at the right spot at the right time."

"You mean the wrong spot at the wrong time," I say.

He laughs. "Where's your glass half full, Kins? This mistake is going to get you what you want."

Mistake.

He's right. It was a mistake, and even though I know it, I'm not sure why hearing him say it loud and clear bothers me. "I never knew you were all the lemons make lemon juice."

"I'm not. If you're given lemons, it's tequila time."

I laugh at that, and hold my head. "I am never drinking tequila again."

"We're going to have to get you a better ring," he says.

My hands drop and I examine the school ring on my finger. "You don't have to do that. I don't want you spending any money on me."

"It's my money, I can spend it any way I want."

"Are we about to have our first fight as a married couple?" I ask with a shaky laugh, still not convinced this is a good idea. Pretending to be married, well technically, we're not pretending, but playing house with a guy like him is every girl's dream. He might be closed off, might say the wrong things, but I am definitely not immune to his charm. This can go sideways on me so fast, go wrong in so many ways that I could lose something far more valuable than my trust fund if this goes off the rail.

"Come on," he says, his voice softer. "If we're doing this, we're doing it right. We're either all in or we're not."

"I guess I'm all in."

"Okay, let's get dressed, and go talk to the others. Then we'll get you a proper ring."

"Look at you, showing your true sides now that we're married. If I'd known you were going to be such a bossy husband, I might not have married you," I say and go perfectly still. Wow, I kind of like the sound of *husband* on my tongue.

He slaps my ass and I yelp. "Easy there, wife," he says. "Or I'll tie you up and show you just how bossy I can really be."

I go still again and he laughs. "Oh my God, you like that idea." I blink at him all innocent like. "I like you more by the minute, Kins," he says and my stupid heart misses a beat.

"What's not to like?" I say to cover that ridiculous emotional reaction. He smiles and is about to turn when I touch his arm. "Cason."

"Yeah." His eyes are warm as they narrow in on me.

"I really want to thank you for this. It means a lot."

He makes a fist and nudges my chin. "Anything for a friend. Now come on. Let's go shock our friends."

We both dress and head down to the restaurant where we find everyone seated around a round table for brunch.

"About time you two got here. What's been taking you so

long?" Liam asks with a smirk and Cason rolls his eyes at his friend.

"If you want to know," Cason says and pulls me in. "Kinsley and I got married last night."

Gasps fill the room as all jaws drop to the table.

"Are you serious?" Nina, his sister says, as his best friend Cole opens and closes his mouth like he can't find his words.

Jules nudges Rider. "Catching the bridal bouquet works magic, huh?"

"Not really," I say. "It was kind of a mistake."

"Oh, another mistake," Liam says and Cason casts him a glance that screams shut up all over it. I'm not sure what the two are talking about but when everyone around the two starts asking a million questions, I hold my hand up to quiet them and take a seat. Cason sits beside me and we flip over our coffee mugs. We stay quiet, keeping the gang in suspense as the server fills our cups and takes our orders.

"Spill already," Nina says, leaning in all conspiratorial like, staring at her brother, her eyes big, like she's eager to hear the details.

"Okay, we didn't think it was real," I begin.

"Elvis was performing on the street. Someone told us it was fake," Cason adds. "Plus, there was tequila involved."

"Lots of tequila," I add.

"Yeah, I'm guessing you never would have done it otherwise," Jonah, aka, the Body Checker pipes in, his wife Quinn smiling at us, like she knows a secret we don't. Actually, many of our friends are giving us that same smile. What's that all about?

"No, of course, we wouldn't," I say and Cason flinches, but when I angle my head his way, he's seated and relaxed, sipping his coffee. I must have mistaken the flinch. He doesn't want this to be real any more than I do. I mean, I don't want it to be real, right?

Oh, crap.

"You're getting it annulled then?" Cole asks.

"Not just yet," Cason says. "We're going to stay married for thirty days, I'm going to help Kinsley out with something personal, then after that, we'll get it annulled."

Cole pushes back in his chair and grins. "Thirty days, huh?" he asks, like he doesn't believe it for a second and once again my stomach tightens. He doesn't seem confident that Cason can hold out that long.

"That's right," Cason says.

Samantha gives me a sweet smile. I don't know her very well, but I think I'd like her. She and Zander, aka The Hard Hitter, live in Boston. "I think you two make a cute couple," she says.

"Technically we're not a couple," I correct and smile. "But yeah, we're cute together." I nudge Cason playfully.

"Can we count on you guys to keep this a secret, and really act like we've suddenly fallen in love and the marriage is legit?" He pinches the bridge of his nose. "Wait, I mean, it is legit, but it's not legit, you know."

"That's our Cason. Always as clear as mud," Cole says.

Cason shoves him and the two get into a pushing match, and I smile, loving the camaraderie between all these hockey players. The wives ignore them for the most part.

"Does this fake marriage come with all the perks?" Jules asks.

I don't answer. I don't need to. The heat racing to my cheeks is a dead giveaway.

"You go, girl," Katee, Luke's wife says.

I turn to hide my blush, even though it's too late, and that's when my gaze lands on Emily. She'd been quiet but now, with her worried gaze on mine, a burst of unease goes down my spine.

She sets her napkin down and stands. "I have to go to the little girl's room."

I take the hint. "I'll join you," I say.

We hurry to the back of the big, busy restaurant and once inside, she puts her arms on my shoulders.

"My God, Kins, what is going on? For real."

"It's okay," I say. "We really did accidently get married, and I suggested we get an annulment right away, but Cason offered to stay married to me so I could get my trust fund."

She gives a low, slow whistle. "That's a big offer."

"I know. He's a nice guy."

I turn to the sink to wash my hands—anything to get away from her probing eyes. But I catch her reflection in the mirror. Christ, I can't get anything by her.

"Kins..." she begins softly. "You like him."

"Of course, I like him." I give a casual shrug, not about to tell her he's been the star of my fantasies for many months now. "He's nice and he's doing me a big favor."

"No, Kins, you like him, like him. It's easy to tell from the way you look at him, and it's also easy to tell you guys have been sleeping together. You both have sex written all over you."

Well, shit.

"We are married," I joke, even though my stomach is so tight, the coffee I sipped earlier is threatening to make an appearance.

"Are you sure you know what you're doing?"

"Yes," I lie.

"He doesn't do relationships, you know that," she says gently. "He never makes it past the two-week mark. It's a running joke between his friends and the puck bunnies."

"We talked about that. It's different this time, though. We're not trying for a relationship. We both know where we stand."

"Do you really, Kins? Do you know where you stand? What you're really getting yourself into with Cason?"

"Perfectly," I say, that lie spilling easily from my lips. I don't really know, but I mean how hard can it be to play house and enjoy the benefits that come with marriage for thirty days? "I'll get my trust fund out of this," I tell her.

"Yeah, but what will you lose in the process?"

The question is a good one. Am I really going to barter with my heart? Will money in *my* palm, and my heart in *Cason*'s be worth the trade off?

I guess we're going to find out.

9

CASON

"Relax, we got this," I say to Kinsley as she anxiously waits for me to finish dressing. We've been back for two days now and we're ready to meet her parents for dinner and drinks.

I take in her light blue dress, the way it flares around her gorgeous thighs, and consider the best way to remove it from her body later.

"My father is good at seeing through a lie, Cason. There's a reason he's one of Seattle's best defense attorneys."

I work the buttons on my dress shirt and step up to her. She's so fidgety I put my hands on her shoulders to settle her. "We're not lying. We really are married, remember?"

"I know, but..."

"No buts. We got this." I dip my head and press my lips to hers. She looks a little startled as I kiss her.

"What was that for?" she asks, her finger going to her lips.

"No reason. I wanted to. Does a husband have to tell his wife why he wants to kiss her?"

"No, I guess not," she says, and holds her hand out to examine her diamond ring. I fiddle with the band on my finger. At first I wasn't going to bother, but then realized to make this authentic, I'd need a ring, too. Here I thought it would deter women from approaching, but oddly enough it seems to draw in more, and that's just wrong. I'm definitely a one-woman kind of guy—even if it is only for two weeks.

"Is it bothering you?" Kins asks and I glance at her.

"Is what bothering me?"

"The ring, you keep fiddling with it."

"No, it's fine. I'm just not used to it."

"Well don't get too used to it. It comes off in a few weeks," she says and I clench down on my jaw at the reminder. "Although you might want to leave it on. It's odd how it's a chick magnet. What is with women wanting what other women have?"

"I'm not a cheater, Kinsley."

"Same," she says.

Just then my cell rings, and I grab it off my nightstand. "It's Cole. I'm going to grab this, okay?"

"Sure, I need to reapply my lipstick. You keep messing it up. But I like it." As she leaves the room, I slide my finger across the screen and step up to my mirror.

"What's up?" I ask and wipe her lipstick from my lips.

"We're all thinking of going to the cottages this weekend. You guys coming or have you already gotten a divorce?" he asks with a chuckle.

"Not funny and I'm not sure. I'll check with Kinsley. She works seven days a week on her truck so I'm not sure she can get the time off."

A long pause and then, "You really doing this, Cason? You're going to stay married to her for one whole month?"

"I'm helping out a friend, so yeah, I'm doing this whole thirty-day thing." I hear pool balls in the background.

"You guys at Nelly's?" I ask. It's our favorite bar, and

tonight is pool night, but I begged off. Guess the guys are all together making plans for the weekend.

"Is he coming?" I hear Liam ask.

Cole covers the phone to say something, then I hear. "Man, he's pussy whipped already."

"Tell him to fuck off," I say.

"I will, then I'll beat his ass at a game just to really piss him off." He goes quiet for a second.

"What's on your mind, Cole?"

"Just ah, you don't think you'll bolt after two weeks? You know as well as I do as soon as a girl gets serious, you're gone."

I fist my hair. It's not quite like that. I leave before they can get serious and I hurt them. "We're not trying to get serious here. We're pretending, remember?"

"Still, I bet you can't make it for the whole month, without her falling for you, and you hurting her by saying the wrong thing."

"I'll make it, and she's the last person I want to hurt, Cole." I lift my eyes to make sure she's not at my door listening.

"You'll take the bet then?"

"Sure, I'll take it," I say, since he keeps pushing the idea. "What are you putting up?"

"What do you want?" Cole asks. It shouldn't piss me off that he thinks this bet is a sure thing for him. Two weeks *is* my record for a reason, but this is different. We're not trying to build something, and she's not going to fall for me, right?

Ah, but the real question is, are you going to fall for her?

Shit.

"How about your precious 69, Dodge Hemi Coronet," I say. I grin. I can just picture the surprised look spreading across his face. I guess he didn't expect me to put that on the table.

"Whoa, are you serious?"

"You want to bet, we bet big."

"Fine then, my Dodge Hemi it is. What are you putting up if you don't follow through?"

"I don't date for a month."

"Make it six."

"Fine, six," I say. I've got this with Kinsley. Yes, I like her and we're having great sex, but I can't fall for her, and no way is she going to fall for me. I can't let her. I'll only hurt her in the end like I do with everyone else.

"Six what?" Kinsley says, poking her head back into the room.

"Oh, nothing. Just a stupid bet Cole and I made." I shove my phone into my back pocket. "Ready?"

She steps up to me and puts her hand on my chest. "Yes, but I'm dreading it."

I put my arm around her and lead her outside, to my sports car in the driveway. Soon I'll have Cole's precious car next to it. I grin as I think about that.

"Something funny?"

"Nope, ah, I forgot to mention, everyone is going to the cottage on the weekend. Great spot on Watauga Beach. I have a cottage there."

"Oh, how nice."

"Do you want to come? It's fun, with all the families and kids, and dogs."

"It actually sounds like fun, but me taking two vacations in one month, or one year is pretty much unheard of."

Disappointment settles in my stomach. "Yeah, I get it."

"But you know, my new assistant is working out pretty good, and maybe I can arrange it."

I smile, and she returns it. "Great, I'll let the others know. You're going to love it." I spend the next fifteen minutes telling her all about the cottages, the water, and fishing and shopping.

"You really like it there, huh?"

"I get to spend time with my two nephews, and all the kids get along. We have a big bonfire every night, and there will be s'mores."

"Cason, you should have opened with that," she says, and I laugh.

When it dies down, she says, "My father can be pretty intimidating. You should probably know that, and that he's probably going to interrogate you. I'm sorry in advance."

"It's okay. I've been up against some pretty intimidating guys on the ice. I think I can handle your father."

"Okay," she says, sounding unconvinced. "We should only have to have this one dinner. They both work twenty-four seven, so I won't have to ask more than this from you."

"I don't mind."

A few minutes later I park at the restaurant, and we exit my car. She glances around the lot. "I think we're early, which is good. I'll need a drink or ten for this."

"Tequila?" I tease.

"Hell, no. That's what got us into this mess in the first place."

"But we're making the best of it," I say and put my arm around her. She relaxes into me, like she's seeking my comfort and I'm happy to give it to her. I actually hate that her parents expect her to live the life they want for her, instead of living it the way she wants and on her terms. I'd tell them to stuff their damn trust fund. But I have money in my bank, and she doesn't, so I'm going to help her out the best way I can.

Her body grows stiffer as we approach the door, and I give her a little squeeze to let her know I'm here. She smiles up at me, as I open the door to the posh Italian restaurant and usher her in.

"Nice place," I say when we enter.

"Mom's favorite," she tells me as a hostess checks our names and leads us to our table. Drink menus are placed in front of us, but before we can open them, her parents come in behind us.

"Dad, Mom," she says and stands to give them the world's most awkward hug. All eyes turn to me when they break apart and I stand for the introduction. "This is Cason Callaghan. My husband. Cason, this is my Dad and Mom, Arthur and Lilith." I extend my arm, and her father slides his beefy palm into mine as his eyes narrow in on me.

"Cason Callaghan," he says. "So nice to meet you in person." He gives me a firm shake and pulls his hand away. "I've seen you play."

"Fan of hockey?"

"Actually, no. I only looked you up after my daughter kindly informed me, over the phone nonetheless, that she married you."

Alright then. "Well it's nice to finally meet you, Mr. Palmer." I wait for him to tell me to call him by his first name. He is, after all, my father-in-law, but the offer doesn't come. I turn my attention to Kinsley's mother. Her lips are pressed tight, forming a thin pink line. "It's nice to meet you Mrs. Palmer."

"Likewise, I'm sure."

Wow, tough crowd.

I sit down next to Kinsley and put my hand on her thigh, and she grasps it in her sweaty palm. My entire body clenches, hating that she's so nervous about this.

"So, hockey." Her father focuses in on me. "How do your parents feel about that?" he asks

"Supportive. Hockey is my passion, and they supported

that all through my life. I wouldn't be a professional without them."

I can almost hear him rolling his eyes in his mind, not at all impressed by my career choice, like chasing a puck around the ice is a child's game. But I make a good living and I'm willing to help his daughter—my wife—out when she needs the help.

Kinsley sits up a little straighter. "They won the Stanley Cup this year, Dad." I take in the eagerness in her eyes as she stares up at her father. After everything, she's still seeking his approval, but this time it's for me. I don't need it. Nor do I want it.

"And that is impressive?" he asks.

I almost laugh at that, but that wouldn't do Kinsley any good. "I guess not," I say. "What's impressive is Kinsley's skills in the kitchen."

"Yes, she makes a great taco. So we've heard," her mom says, a hint of disgust attached to her words.

My jaw drops. "Are you saying you've never tasted them, never eaten at her truck?"

"We don't eat at trucks, dear," Lilith says.

"You're definitely missing out."

"It's okay," Kinsley says quietly. "They don't like street food."

"Maybe not, but I bet they'll love your new restaurant food. The place is going to be cozy, inviting, and have sit down tables with service." Kinsley's body goes so tight, I'm worried she's going to snap something. What the hell?

"What's this about a new restaurant?" her father asks, and my heart drops. Shit, was I not supposed to mention that? Fuck me. Here I go saying the wrong things again.

"It's something I want to do in the future, Dad," she says, and reaches for her water glass. Her diamond sparkles in the overhead light.

Her mother lifts her chin to see it. "That's the ring?"

"It is. Isn't it beautiful," Kinsley says as she examines it.

"Lovely, dear. Perfect for a Vegas wedding. I suppose Elvis was there?" She gives a humorless laugh. "Your grandmother would have loved that."

Wow, shitty fucking parents.

"It was a last minute thing, Mom. A spur of the moment decision."

Lilith gives a glare of disapproval. "Yes, you're very good at those."

I put my arm around Kinsley. "I couldn't wait one more second to make her my bride."

"Why, is she pregnant?" her father asks, and my temper flares. Is he fucking serious? The disrespect they have for Kinsley makes me want to pummel something. What the fuck is wrong with them?

"No, I'm not pregnant."

"Thank God for that," her father bursts out.

"Don't you want grandkids?" I ask.

The server comes back and we all give our drink order. When we're alone again, her mother says, "Kinsley's made enough mistakes."

I take a deep breath, and hold it for a second, hoping it will extinguish the fire brewing in my belly. How the hell can they be so rude to their daughter? I shift a little closer to her, and present a united front.

"Not in my eyes. I think Kinsley is living her dream life."

She smiles up at me, and my heart pinches tight. "It's important to follow your passion, don't you think?" I ask her parents.

Instead of answering, her mother says, "We'll have a proper reception in our garden. I'll make the arrangements." She looks at me. "Your parents will come, I assume."

I shift, a bit uncomfortable. "Well, they'll probably be away," I say. "They vacation in the Med this time of year."

She stares at me for a second, like she's not sure whether she believes me or not, then says, "Siblings and friends?"

I nod. "I have a sister and Kinsley and I have many friends."

"Fine, I'll get the invitations made up and you see to it that they land in the hands of those you'd like to attend."

"We don't need—" Kinsley begins, and her mother cuts her off.

"You ran off and got married, Kinsley. How do you think that looks to our family and friends?"

"When you're in love, you're in love," I say. "I talked her into it."

"Then talk her into a proper reception," her father says. He looks at Kinsley over his glasses. "That's hardly an act that proves you're a grown up."

"I am a grown up, Dad. I'm twenty-six years old."

"Your actions speak louder than words, don't you think?"

"I actually do think that's true," I say. "Our actions proved we love each other, and couldn't wait to be married."

Her father practically dismisses me when he says, "Yes, well. Let's see how long that lasts."

Just. Wow.

I'd take my parents and their lack of affection, and lack of interest in my life over these two any day. My heart goes out to Kinsley. No one should ever be treated the way they're treating her.

"I think a reception is a great idea," I say, and Kinsley's eyes widen.

"You do?" she asks quietly.

"Of course." I bring her hand to my mouth and kiss it.

"You don't have—"

"I want to."

Our drinks come and I'd like to down the scotch in one mouthful. Instead, I sip it, since I don't want to be judged any more than I am. They can do and say what they want about me, but I'm going to defend Kinsley with everything in me.

Her father sits back in his seat, his gaze sliding back and forth between the two of us, a careful assessment. I meet his stare. I'm sure in the courthouse he's an intimidating man, but he doesn't scare me. I think he's a big fucking bully and I don't like bullies.

"You know," he begins. "Evan made partner at the firm. He's doing quite well for himself."

"Yes, he's doing great things," her mother says.

"Good for him," Kinsley says, her chin high.

"When was the last time you two talked?"

"We don't talk. We're over. He broke it off with me, remember?"

"Yes, well, you surprised us all, Kinsley. What was he supposed to do?"

"Support her," I pipe in.

"I believe he was just trying to give you a wakeup call," her father says.

"Do you think him telling me I wasn't special was a wakeup call? He was only with me to climb the ladder, Dad," She counters, her voice rising an octave, her frustration written all over her face.

"He just didn't want you to get off course." Her mother casts me a quick glance. "If you get back on it…"

No way. No fucking way. They're really sitting here trying to get Kinsley back with her asshole ex while her husband is right here beside her—supporting her.

Fuck this shit.

"Lucky for me they never worked out. Now I get to call this beautiful woman my wife."

"We're very happy," Kinsley says as her parents glare at her.

"Oh, we're definitely happy," I say. "I plan to do whatever it takes to put a smile on Kinsley's face."

For the next few weeks, anyway.

10

KINSLEY

"I am so sorry," Cason says when we step outside.

I glance up at him and frown as he shakes his head, incredulously. "You're sorry. What do you have to be sorry about? You did well in there, and I'm the one who should be sorry for subjecting you to them."

"Kins," he says. "They're your parents, I get it, but man, they really don't respect your choices. I'm sorry for that."

I glance at my feet. "I know. I'm a huge disappointment to them."

He touches my chin and lifts it an inch. "Are you disappointed in yourself?"

"No."

"Remember this. A lot of people won't see your worth. Just make sure you're not one of them."

My heart beats a little faster. "Thanks, Cason. The truth is, I love what I do, but..." I put my hand on my stomach, to soothe the ache that always flares after spending time with my parents. "It hurts that they care more about my image and how it affects the family, than my well-being." A car door closes, and I briefly look away. "You don't have to go through with the reception. I'll figure out a way for us to get out of it."

"Like hell. I'm going. I'm not going to let them get the better of us by not showing and giving them something else to throw back in your face."

My gaze flies back to his. "Cason—"

"Are we about to have our second argument, Mrs. Kinsley Elizabeth Palmer-Callaghan?" he asks playfully.

I laugh. "No. I'm tapping out. You always seem to get your way somehow."

"I plan to have my way with you later. But I just want to say, let's go through with it, let's charm the pants off your parents and their friends. We'll show them how happy you are with your decisions and the direction of your life."

The thing is, I actually am happy. Happy with my food truck, my plans for a restaurant. Happy when I'm with Cason. But I'd be wise to remember what this is and what this isn't.

"Want to see something?" I ask and his gaze drops to my chest. The heat in his eyes trickles through me, and awakens all my girly parts.

"Ah, yeah. Did you not hear me when I said I plan to have my way with you?"

I whack him. "I'm not talking about my boobs, Cason."

"Jeez, is that all you think about, Kinsley?" He feigns exasperation. "I wouldn't have married you if I'd known you were a sex addict."

"Puh-lease, that would have gotten you to the altar faster," I shoot back.

He laughs. "Okay, what do you want to show me? Although nothing will live up to my expectations now."

"How about the space I want for my restaurant? Will that be a good second?"

"Actually, yeah. I'd love to see it."

"Let's head to Pike's Place."

We hurry to his car, and the sun is low on the horizon as we drive downtown and find parking. The market is closing up, vendors putting their fares away for another day by the time we arrive.

"How about we hop on the Seattle Wheel. Take a look at the city from the sky."

I laugh. He knows full well I'm afraid of heights, but I always do end up enjoying myself. "It's like you don't know me at all."

"I'm actually enjoying getting to know you better."

"I'm enjoying getting to know you better too, although your life is an open book, Cason. They write about you in the papers enough."

"Don't believe everything you read," he says as we walk the downtown streets.

"Right here," I say and slide my hand into his to drag him around the corner. We come across a newly renovated building, merely a few blocks from the waterfront. I smile up at Cason, then peer into the window. He stands next to me, the scent of his freshly showered skin teasing my senses.

"This is it, huh?" he asks.

I nod. "I think it's perfect. I honestly can't even believe it hasn't been rented yet. It's such an amazing location." I step back. "I can almost see my sign hanging right over the door."

"Have you been inside?" he asks.

"No." I crinkle my nose. "I don't want to get myself too excited, you know."

He shrugs. "It wouldn't hurt to just look."

"Yeah, maybe."

He looks into the window. "I guess I owe you an apology."

My head snaps up. "For what?"

"I opened my big mouth and mentioned the restaurant to

your parents. I told you, I have a knack for saying the wrong things."

"It's okay." I nudge him playfully. "You can make it up to me later."

A wide smile lights up his handsome face. "My pleasure."

"Mine, too," I say and chuckle.

He shoves his hands into his pockets, his eyes narrowing in on me. "How come you didn't want them to know?"

"I think they still hold out hope that I'll fail at this and realize I need to go back to law school. I can't even believe they brought up Evan, right in front of you, like now that he's a partner, I'll go running back to him."

"That was a douche move, for sure, and you won't fail at this Kinsley."

I smile. "I love your faith in me."

"I've eaten your food. It's amazing."

"Wait, did you just call my folks douches?"

"Sorry."

I laugh. "Maybe it's your honesty that gets you into trouble."

"It could be. I probably shouldn't have said that. You mad?"

"No, and I know my food is good, I just hope my truck holds together for a little while longer." I turn back to the restaurant. "I'd rather put the money into this, over the truck."

"Tell me how you'd design it," he says, and I love the interest on his face. It's real and genuine, and for a minute makes me forget that while we're actually married, we're in a pretend relationship.

I throw my hands up and animatedly tell him everything I want to do. From sourcing locally, with the market being so close, to helping those living on the streets. This is such a perfect location for that.

Taking me by surprise, Cason scoops me up and spins me around. "I love seeing you this excited," he says, and when we stop spinning his lips close over mine. His kisses are sweet and passionate and my whole body responds.

By the time my feet hit the ground, I'm breathless, and aroused, and anxious to get him naked. My God, I really like this guy. I have no idea how I'm going to give him up after our month together. I only know that I have to. He's only on loan to me, but while I have him, I damn well plan to take advantage of every minute.

"Home, now," I whisper, and he puts his arm around me.

"No Seattle Wheel?"

"I want to go for a ride, Cason. But not on the wheel."

He laughs at that and we hurry back to his car. "My place or yours?" he asks as we slide into our seats and buckle up.

"Mine, it's closer, and I want you naked."

"I said it once and I'll say it again. I do love a girl who knows what she wants."

Love.

My heart leaps, and I work to settle it. If he knew how much I liked hearing that word on his tongue—he'd likely run. It was a mistake that brought us together, and a mistake for me to think he really means what he says. I mean, he did warn me about that.

Oh, God, I am going to be in so much trouble when this is over.

He guns his sports car and I laugh to shake off the things I shouldn't be feeling. "You're going to get a speeding ticket and that is just going to slow us down."

"You're right." He eases off the pedal, and I reach over, putting my hand over his thick cock. I rub him gently, and he swallows hard.

"Jesus," he moans under his breath, and I open his pants and slide my hand inside. His knuckles grip the wheel harder.

"Keep that up and I'm going to hit a lamppost," he says, and I can't help but grin. I love the way he gets so hard for me.

I ease my hand out. "That will just slow us down, too," I say, as I sit tight until he pulls up to my place. We both hurry from the car, and into my small condo. It's not much compared to his mansion, but it's mine, and I'm proud of what I've accomplished so far.

Inside, he kicks my door shut, and the blatant display of alpha behavior teases the needy spot between my legs. There's just something about a manly man. Then again, maybe there's just something about Cason.

He takes both of my hands, puts them over my head, and backs me up until I'm against the door, captive between his hard body—and the man is hard everywhere—and the door. He uses his knee to widen my legs, and when he puts it against my sex, I move against it, shamelessly rubbing myself on him.

"Fuck, you are sexy," he moans into my mouth as he kisses me.

"Want to know what you are?" I murmur back.

"What?" he asks, his mouth going to my neck. I angle for him, and his tongue leaves a wet streak as he makes his way to my breasts.

"Overdressed," I say, and he chuckles.

The next thing I know I'm in his arms, and he's taking me upstairs to my bedroom. Once again he kicks the door shut behind us.

He backs up and starts unbuttoning his shirt. I wet my lips, loving this sexy little removal of clothes. With a roll of his broad shoulder, he shrugs from the shirt and it falls to his feet.

"Keep going," I say and point to his pants, the button still open from earlier.

The hiss of his zipper fills the space between us, and my

pulse jumps in anticipation. He makes quick work of his pants and stands before me in his boxers, his erection straining for freedom.

I step up to him, and drop to my knees. "Remember the first time I took your cock into my mouth?" I ask, working hard to forget he thought he was with Emily that night.

He puts his hand on my face as I free his pulsing cock. It pulses against my chin. I stick my tongue out and lightly lick around his crown, and a tortured sound crawls out of his throat.

"How could I ever forget that?"

"I was wondering about something."

"What?" he asks, and pushes my hair from my face.

"You couldn't see me, so I was wondering if it was better in the dark, or is it hotter if you can watch me take you into my mouth." I lean forward and take him deep, until he's hitting the back of my throat, and his hands fist my hair. He swells inside my mouth, his soft curses urge me on.

"This," he says. "Fuck, Kins. Watching you take my cock like this is the hottest thing I've ever seen." I back up a bit, and he plops from my mouth. Pre-cum drips from his slit, and I stick my tongue out again, and he drips on it. "Holy fuck," he says.

I swallow him and give his crown a lick to get every drop. "Mmm," I say. "I love the taste of you."

"You are so good at that," he says.

"I never used to like it."

"You like it now, Kins? You like my cock?" he asks, the hitch in his voice bringing my gaze to his. The want, need, and desire I see reflecting in his eyes, caresses every inch of my body.

"Yeah, Cason. I like doing this to you," I say honestly. I blink up at him, teasing slightly, as I say. "Are you done with the questions so I can get back to your cock?"

"Fuck," he says and grips my hair tighter to guide my mouth back to his raging erection. "No more questions." I take him deep again and his hips canter forward, until his crown is in my throat. "I love watching you suck on me." He throbs in my mouth, and I sense he's close. I take his balls into my hand and massage lightly. "Kins," he groans. "I'm too close." He tries to pull me off him, but I refuse to let him. I bob my head, my lips tight around his cock. When he gets the idea that I want him to come in my mouth, he loosens his grip on my head, and lets loose a deep growl.

I work my mouth over him, and take his base into my hand. I slide back and forth, my hand following the motion as I continue to fondle his balls, and when he stops moving, his labored pants letting me know he's close, I inch back, and hold out my tongue, all the while running my hand up and down his long, thick shaft.

"So fucking hot," he murmurs, and his cock jumps as he spills onto my hungry tongue. He comes and comes and comes some more, his body stiff as he depletes himself. I drink him in, and ever so softly, run my tongue over his crown to taste all of him.

"You are incredible," he groans and reaches for me. He pulls me to my feet, and he looks a bit dazed and lost as his eyes move over my face. "That was the hottest thing I've ever seen," he says.

"You don't have to say that."

"Why wouldn't I say that when it's true?"

A thrill goes through me. "Still want to watch?" I ask, and he angles his head, like he's wondering where I'm taking this.

"Watch what?"

"This," I say, bold and brazen from his compliment. I release the buttons on my dress and let it fall to the floor. He sucks in a sharp breath as he takes in my matching bra and panties, recently purchased. "You like?" I ask.

"Yeah, I fucking like."

"Does this make up for having to sit through a horrible dinner tonight?"

"It wasn't so horrible because I was with you," he says and my stupid heart does a little dance.

"But you hardly ate."

"Maybe I was saving my appetite," he says, and I grin as his gaze leisurely travels the length of my body, stopping at the juncture of my legs.

"You want to eat my pussy, Cason?"

He groans. "Fuck, yeah." His eyes move back to my face. "You want to watch?"

"There's something I want you to watch first." His cock starts to grow again, expand as I unhook my bra and let it fall. Everything about the way this man watches me boosts my confidence. I don't feel chubby or frumpy under his gaze. The heat in his eyes lets me know I'm beautiful to him, that every curve is worthy of worship.

I put my hand into my panties, and touch myself. "Yes," he murmurs, and I move my hips, stroking my clit and sliding a finger into my tight, wet center. "I want to see," he says. "Take off your panties, spread your lips wide open, and fuck yourself with your finger. Show me how you do it, Kins."

His words race through me and fill me with a new kind of want. I hook my fingers into my lacy band and shimmy them down my hips.

"You are such a tease," he says.

"And you like it."

"I like it," he murmurs and comes closer as I slide my panties off and turn my back to him to reach into my nightstand.

"That's a dangerous thing you're doing, Kins."

I glance at him over my shoulder. "Dangerous how?" I ask but the answer is all over his face as he gazes at my curvy backside. He's such an ass man. I wiggle a bit, and he growls as he closes the distance between us. He takes my ass cheeks into his palms and squeezes. "Never mind," I tell him, and reach into my nightstand.

His hands fall and he stumbles back a bit when I pull out my vibrator.

"Jesus, Kins."

"You still want to watch?"

"More than life," he says, and I nudge him until he's sitting on the edge of my bed. I climb onto the bed on all fours and he curses under his breath as I center myself on the mattress. My little toy buzzes to life as I spread my legs, and run it over my breasts, down my stomach, and between my legs. I moan as I stroke it over my clit. My eyes shut but I force them open.

The look on Cason's face is everything I thought it would be and maybe a bit better. He's loving this as much as I am. That's when it occurs to me that I love pleasing him as much as he loves pleasing me.

I press the vibrator to my opening and slide it in, the buzzing sound now muffled by my walls. I work the toy inside me and when I pull it out it's slick and shiny from my juices.

"Feels so good," I say and run the vibrating end over my engorged clit.

"So good," he agrees, and takes his cock into his hand. He pumps himself with his fist, and I'm shocked that he's hard and rearing to go so soon after coming in my mouth.

My heart races faster as we masturbate in front of each other, but I need more. I need him. I can use my toy anytime and he looks about as ready to be inside me as I am to have him. Our eyes meet, and I telegraph a message without words. He takes a condom from his pocket, climbs between my legs, and takes the vibrator from me. He doesn't toss it away. Instead he uses it on me, sliding it over my clit and sinking it inside me. I grip the bedding and cry out, doing my very best to stave off an orgasm until he's pumping inside me.

"Cason. I want your cock," I cry out.

He rips into the foil with his teeth, and quickly sheathes himself. "Yes," I say, my throat now dry from all my panting. Still buzzing, the vibrator lands on the bed beside me as he falls over me and in one fast, hard thrust, he's inside me, moving, pumping. Hard, blunt strokes that steal my ability to think.

I wrap my hands around him, run my nails over his back, and rake my teeth over his shoulder, marking his body. He slicks in and out of me, creating friction and heat as we move together, each chasing pleasure. His finger finds my clit and that's it for me. I let go, come all over his cock, and he pushes my hair from my face, his lips on mine as he releases with me.

The toy buzzes beside me, the sound a little muffled by our fast breaths. I turn to see my vibrator, and nearly laugh hysterically. Not because any of this is funny. It's not. It's just that my favorite toy will never be enough for me again. Not after Cason.

Damned if that doesn't pose a big freaking problem.

11

CASON

The rustling beside me pulls me awake, and I open one eye and then another. A smile spreads across my face as I watch a naked Kinsley, try to sneak from her bed. It's funny because it's usually me sneaking away before the break of dawn, but I'm married now, so to speak, and in no hurry to go anywhere.

Last night in her bed, she played games with me, touching herself, showing me another side of herself, a private one. I can't even put into words what that was like for me. I honestly don't remember sex ever being so good, so deeply intimate.

Fuck, man, I could get used to this.

I shake my head. What the hell am I saying? We're together so she can get her trust fund and get her life in order. I'm in it for the sex and tacos, and Cole's rare car is the cherry on top. Honestly, he's the one who pushed for the bet, and I'm not sure why, but his car has nothing to do with me wanting to last thirty days. I want to help her. I like her. A lot.

"Where are you going?"

She jumps and spins when she sees me, her hand on her chest. "How long have you been awake?" she asks, her palm pressed to her chest. I hold my hand out, reach for her, needing her naked body next to mine, almost desperately.

"Long enough to see you trying to sneak away."

"I wasn't sneaking away," she says. "I have to go to work."

I wave my fingers, gesturing for her to come to me. "As nice as that sounds, Cason, I have to go. Kat isn't feeling well, so I need to get all the prep work done myself."

I toss the covers off. "No you don't."

She puts one hand on her hip. "Oh, you're going to help me?"

"Of course, I am Mrs. Kinsley Callaghan. Isn't that what good husbands do?"

"I see you've shortened my last name to just yours."

"It was kind of long." That might be true, but maybe I just like hearing my last name attached to her first name, no measure of distance between them. Although if she wants the joint name, I'm okay with that, too. My God, what am I saying? None of this is real. "A bit of a mouthful, don't you think?"

As soon as those words spill from my lips, her gaze drops, takes in my early morning boner. I laugh. "My God, you are such a sex addict." I take my cock into my hand and she groans. "This is the first thing you think of when I say mouthful."

"Yeah, it's bad," she says and we both burst out laughing. "As much as I'd like..." she moves her finger in a circle over the mussed up bed. "to do all this again, I really do need to go."

"All right. Let's do this," I say searching the floor for last night's clothes. "We'll have to stop at my place. I need to change."

"Cason, you don't have to help me. Besides, what do you know about cooking? You're a hockey player."

I step up to her, put my hands on her arms and rub gently. "I actually know a lot, Kins. Nina and I...we had to fend for ourselves a lot. My parents were pretty absent in our lives. I mean they loved us and supported us, but they were both investment bankers with busy jobs that kept them at the office for hours. Nina and I did a lot of the cooking. She was better at it than me, but I definitely know how to help out."

A sadness moves over her face. "I didn't know that, Cason. I'm sorry they weren't more involved in your life."

"It's okay, we both turned out fine."

She frowns like she's not so sure about that, and maybe she's right. Maybe I didn't turn out fine, considering I can't do relationships, can't really express myself properly.

"Do you see them now?"

"Oh, yeah, every now and then. I mean they love us, gave us everything we wanted, pretty much—outside of their time. They'd love you." Shit, I didn't mean to put it that way. "Not that we're going to tell them we're married or anything. No point in that. I don't need a trust fund." She winces and I say, "That's not coming out right, Kinsley."

"It's fine," she says and puts her hand on my chest. "I get it. You're right. There is no sense involving them in this sham of a marriage." She blinks and her brow pulls together when she asks, "What did you mean they gave you everything you wanted, pretty much?"

Wanting to put a smile back on her face again, I say, "Don't tell anyone, but when I was young, I secretly wanted an Easy Bake Oven."

She smiles. "Really?"

"Yeah, really." I angle my head, take in her expression. "Do you think that's strange?"

"No. I don't. I think it's great. You know Bobby Flay had one growing up, right?"

"No, I didn't. But I dig it."

"Did you ever ask for one?"

"My parents put me in hockey, they put Nina in figure skating. Very gender defined roles. I just knew it would be frowned upon if I asked for what they would consider a 'girl's' toy. Sad, but true. That's how it was in their generation. Change is slow, but it's coming."

"My son is getting an easy bake oven, and my daughter is getting a hockey stick," she says with a tip of her chin.

"This coming from the anti-marriage girl?"

She looks at her ring. "A little too late for that isn't it?"

I brush the back of my knuckles over her cheek. "It's never too late for anything, Kins."

She throws her hands up in the air. "Parents," she teases, lightening the mood. "They sure know how to do a number on us."

She's not wrong. "Do you think your parents believed we were legit?"

"They saw the ring, and Mom wants to throw a party so I think they believed us. What's not to believe, we really are married."

"Okay, let's get moving." I bend to give her a fast kiss, but it grows, expands, blossoms into something deeper, something warm and affectionate. We both take a fast breath when we part, and I say, "If we don't go now, I'm going to toss you onto that bed and have my way with you."

Passion and indecision dances in her eyes. "Can I have a raincheck?"

"Kiss me like that again and you can have anything you want," I say.

"Here I thought a way to a man's heart was through his stomach." As soon as the words leave her mouth, she shakes her head. "Not that I'm looking for your heart, Cason. What I meant to say—"

I put my finger to her lush lips. "It's fine, now let's get moving."

"Right," she says. "I'm going to have a fast shower."

"I'll put on the coffee."

I find my clothes and dress as she hurries to the shower. Downstairs I get the coffee going and pull my phone from my pants. I do a quick search on the property she's interested in and make sure she's not coming down the stairs when I make a call. I want to surprise her with this.

"I'm all set," she says. "Oh, sorry. I didn't mean to interrupt." She eyes my phone as I turn from her, not wanting her to hear the tail end of my conversation.

"Yeah, I'll be there," I say to the manager of the building. I end the call and shove the phone in my pocket.

"Everything okay?" she asks.

"Fine."

She jerks her thumb toward the door. "Do you have somewhere to be?"

"Yeah, my place so I can shower quickly and change."

She hesitates for a second, a frown on her face, and I get it. Her douchebag ex walked out on her, and left her a little broken. But I'm not going anywhere. Not for the rest of the month, anyway.

"C'mon," I say and capture her hand.

Forty minutes later, after a fast stop at the market to get all her fresh ingredients, we're inside the tight quarters of her food truck. I kind of like the way we keep bumping into one another.

"So this is what it's like back here."

She grins. "Hot, tight, and slippery—"

I groan to cut her off and she closes her mouth and gives

me the side eye. "Stop, you're turning me on," I say and adjust my cock in my jeans.

She laughs and puts her hand on my chest. "Slippery if you're not wearing the right shoes, and you're not, so don't fall, because I can't afford a lawsuit."

"I'll be careful." I glance around. "What do you want me to do first?"

"Okay," she says going into professional chef mode. "We need to get all the vegetables prepared." She checks her watch. "We open in an hour, and that's when things really get rolling."

I dig into the box to pull out the produce and spend the next hour washing, cutting, and filling the trays. Beside me, Kinsley cooks and prepares all the meat. It's amazing watching her work, doing what she loves most. How can her folks not see that this is where she belongs? Well, she actually belongs in her own restaurant and damned if I'm not going to help that happen.

"Want to play a game," I say.

She flips the chicken. "Working here, Cason."

"We can work and play."

"What do you want to play?" she asks, her focus only half on me.

"How about two truths and a lie."

She chuckles and the sound wraps around my chest and squeezes tight. Man, I love seeing her happy like this. I want to put a smile like that on her face every day.

"Are you twelve?" she asks.

"You'll play then?"

"Fine. I'll go first. Let me think." She removes the chicken from the grill, and goes quiet, lost in thought as she grabs a sponge and washes down the dirty dishes. "Okay, when I was young my sisters hung me from the clothesline. Two, I had an aversion to pizza during my teen years." My head jerks back. I can't believe that. All teenagers love pizza, don't they?

"And three?"

"And three, I never knew sex could be so good until Vegas."

I puff my chest up. "I know that's not a lie."

"Maybe that's the lie. Maybe I'm playing into that huge ego of yours."

"Nah, it's true. I tasted you and felt you squeeze around my fingers and cock, remember?" I say, and she goes bright red as she tosses a wet sponge at me. I grab it and set it back in the sink. "I'm going to go with, hung from the clothesline."

"Wrong," she says. "They did and I fell and it hurt like hell."

"No way." That's like child abuse. "Where the hell were your parents?"

"Working, of course. My sisters were supposed to be taking care of me."

"Seems like we have working parents in common. But I was a lot nicer to Nina than your sisters were to you."

"Yup, they locked me in a suitcase once. It's a wonder I'm not claustrophobic. I don't see them much anymore. They both work in Manhattan now. I'm their only daughter left here in Seattle, and if my parents continue to pressure me about my choices, they're going to drive me away, too." She shakes her head. "Okay, now you."

"All right. When I was young, I wanted to be a police officer."

"Hmm," she says.

"Two, I lost my virginity at fourteen, with Josee Fraser, in her parent's basement. I think we were watching Veronica Mars."

"Truth," she says. "Although I would have guessed thirteen, and just so you know, most times when people give too much detail it usually means they're lying."

"Look at the lawyer in you coming out." I laugh and give her hair a little tug.

"Okay, what's your third?"

"You're the most beautiful woman I've ever met."

Her cheeks turn a pretty shade of pink, much like her hair. "Thanks, Cason," she says. "Sometimes you know, you really do say the right things."

"Maybe that's the lie," I tease.

"You jerk," she says and throws the sponge at me again. This time I'm ready so I dodge it and pull her into my arms for a kiss. "I never wanted to be a cop," I say. "I wanted to be a hockey player since the day I was born."

"And you are, and that is so amazing, Cason."

"And you're a chef. You'll get what you want too, babe."

I let her go, and we go back to preparing food, and talk about nothing and everything, and it's weird how natural it feels being with her like this.

"It's go time," she says once we have all the food prepared, and goes about opening the truck. I stand back and take in the whole process from inside the truck instead of outside on the sidewalk.

Soon enough the crowds form, and she gives me a quick rundown on how to prepare the burrito bowls. The two of us work together in sync, like it's something we've always done, and once we got the lunch crowd served, we start the whole process over for the dinner crowd.

"You know this is kind of fun," I say as I stuff my face with a chicken taco.

"It is, isn't it?"

"I love watching you work, and damn these are good." I hold it out to her and she takes a generous bite.

"That was a mouthful," I say, teasing her from our earlier conversation.

She chuckles and sauce spills down her chin, and I slide my finger over it. "So messy."

She leans against the counter, and an overhead fan nearly falls on her head. I move quickly to grab it. "Shit, Kins. That would have hurt."

She frowns. "I know, I fixed it once, but the screws keep coming out."

"I'll fix it for you," I say and examine the screws. "Do I have time to make it to the hardware store before you open again?"

"I can open without you. I ran this truck for months on my own." She sighs. "You've done enough, Cason. You don't have to come back."

I pull her into my arms, my groin pressed against her stomach. "Don't want me?"

"Oh, I want you. But you don't have to be here. You probably have other more important things to do. I mean, on the phone this morning, not that I was trying to listen in, but—"

"Nothing more important than this," I say, and her protest dies an abrupt death when my lips close over hers.

"Get a room already," someone on the sidewalk says, and we turn to find Cole and Nina standing there, with my two awesome nephews, Brandon and Casey, named after me, of course.

"Hey guys," I say, and lean over the counter.

"What are you doing uncle Cason?" Brandon asks, as he frowns up at me.

"Helping out a friend. You guys want a taco?" I ask.

Nina glances at Kinsley. "Is he being a nuisance? He was always underfoot in the kitchen growing up."

Kinsley laughs. "He's been pretty good, actually."

"Hear that Neaner-Neaner," I say to piss her off and she glares at me.

"The tacos are on uncle Cason, boys," Nina says. "Drinks, too. Order whatever you want."

I laugh at that. "A dozen tacos coming up," I say. "Go grab a seat at the bench, and I'll bring them to you."

As they saunter away, Kinsley and I make the food, and I put it all on a tray. "Come on," I say. "Come sit with us for a bit."

"No, they're your family, Cason. I'm not going to interfere."

"Listen wifey, get your sweet buns off this truck. You've been on your feet all day, and you're taking a break. Husband's orders."

"Fine," she says and takes off her apron. We walk to the picnic table, and I note the way Casey is staring at Kinsley. You never know what's going to come out of the mouth of a two-year-old.

"I like your pink hair," he says, and Kinsley smiles at him.

"Thank you, Casey. I like your t-shirt."

"I like Paw Patrol," he says as I hand out the tacos and napkins.

They all start to eat, and Nina moans. "Kinsley these are so good."

"Excuse me," I say. "I believe I made that one."

Nina rolls her eyes at me and turns to Kinsley. Nina takes her hands. "Your ring is so gorgeous. Mom is going to love it."

"Oh, we're not telling your parents," Kinsley says, and Nina frowns. "We don't want them to get the wrong idea."

"Do your parents know?"

"Yeah, because Cason is helping me out with something."

As the two talk, I glance at Cole, note the way he's looking at me, like I'm going to cut and bail anytime now. I resist the urge to give him the middle finger and tell him to fuck off because my nephews are here so I take a different approach.

"How's my Hemi?" I ask, my voice low. "Keeping her nice and clean for me?"

"Yours? It's not yours," Brandon says. Jesus, that kid doesn't miss a thing.

I nudge him. "I know buddy, just playing with your Dad."

"You're going to come then?" Nina asks Kinsley, and I turn my focus to them.

"If my assistant is back, yeah, I'd love to. I think it would be fun."

"You talking about the cottage?" I ask.

Nina nods. "Yeah, I'm looking forward to it." She wipes her mouth with a napkin. "So tell me what's going on with you two?"

"You know what's going on with us," I say, even though I'm not exactly sure what's going on with me, because I'm beginning to really like my time with Kins. Beginning to wonder if we could have more after our month together. We're having fun, I know, and I'm not supposed to be having deeper feelings, but dammit if I can help that. Maybe I'm saying the right things, because we were friends first—and a part of me knows she could be the right girl for me. Maybe I won't fuck this up, like I fuck everything else up. Then again, maybe I'm getting ahead of myself. She's anti-marriage, right? But could there be a chance she might want to try for more?

"I want the details. I might be able to use it in a book," she says.

Kinsley laughs. Hard. "No, Nina, your books end with a happily ever after. That's not what's going on here. Cason is just helping me out, then we're done."

At least that answers my question.

12

KINSLEY

"You sure you got this?" I ask, holding my phone to my ear as I pace inside Cason's big mansion. It was just a few days ago Kat called in sick, and here I am asking if she can take over the running of the truck—again. I haven't had a break in a year, working seven days a week, and now here I am taking my second vacation this month, and heading to Cason's cottage—with a handful of wedding receptions for his friends.

"Yes" I got this," Kat says. "I'm feeling perfectly fine now, and Jason is up for giving me a hand. He might only be seventeen, but he's an aspiring chef and this will do him good."

I met her brother Jason. He's a good kid, and I really shouldn't worry so much. My truck will be in good hands, but maybe that's not what I'm worried about though. Maybe I'm worried about going to the lake with Cason, and falling just a little more in love with him. I sigh, and Kat must have misread it.

"Don't you trust me?"

"For sure I do, Kat."

"What's wrong then?"

I lift my gaze when Cason comes into the living room, and my heart beats just a little faster in my chest. He raises his brow, and I nod to let him know the weekend is a go, and Kat is feeling better. He gives me two thumbs up and I chuckle.

"Nothing wrong," I fib. "I really appreciate this, Kat."

"You just remember that when you open your new restaurant, and need an assistant."

I chuckle. "I'm pretty sure there's a promotion for you and a position for Jason."

She lets loose a loud whoop, and I hold the phone away from my ear. "Okay, go. Have fun. We got this."

We end the call, and Cason wraps his arms around me. "Everything in order?"

"All set to go," I say and he angles his head.

"You sure you're okay?"

I plaster on my best smile, and put a rope around my emotions, to rein them bad boys in. Cason puts his big hand on my cheek, the sweeping of his thumb stirring those barely leashed feelings growing inside me.

"Just worried about my truck," I say.

"Understandable. At least we know the fan won't fall and kill anyone."

I follow him to the front door, and he scoops up my duffle bag. There's another bag in the back seat of his car, one I stashed there earlier without him knowing, and it excites me.

"I really appreciate you and Cole doing all that work on the truck. You didn't have to do that. I actually feel kind of bad. This marriage seems so one-sided."

He chuckles. "It's not, but if you really and truly feel that way, this weekend you can show me how appreciative you are."

I laugh at that. "Didn't I do that last night?"

His smile curls through me, warms me from the inside out. "Yeah, you did. But I want more."

God, I want more, too, but not just in the bedroom.

We head outside, the late day sun falls over us, and we climb into his car. "We have to make a pit stop," he says.

"Oh, where?"

"It's a surprise."

I take in his mischievous grin. "I don't like surprises."

"You'll like this one." He reaches for my hand and takes it in his. His warmth shimmers through me, and I smile. Even though I know I'm going to end up heartbroken, I haven't had this much fun in a long time. "You're smiling."

I chuckle. "Something wrong with that?"

"No, Kins. I love when you smile." He turns his focus to the traffic, and I take in the buildings as we hit downtown Seattle.

"What are we doing here?" I ask.

"What part of "it's a surprise" didn't you get?" I pull my hand from his and whack his chest and he lets loose a fake oomph.

A few minutes later he parks, and I stretch out my legs as I climb out. With my hand back in his again, he leads me down the street and when we take the corner I know exactly where we're going. He leads me to the rental space, and I stop at the door.

"Why are we here?" I ask.

He pulls a key from his pocket and jangles it. "Because we're going to check out the space."

I gasp, surprised and a little nervous. "How did you get that?"

"I have connections," he says.

"Really?"

"Well, no," he says and laughs. "But I made a few calls. pulled a few strings, and voila."

"This is what you were up to the other day when I heard

you on the phone?" He nods, and my heart wobbles in my too tight chest. "You are so sweet, Cason."

"Shh," he says and glances around. "I have a reputation to uphold you know. Can't be letting anyone on the ice think otherwise that The Troublemaker isn't going to knock their teeth out if they mess with him or his teammates."

I chuckle but it holds no humor. Nibbling on my bottom lip I back up an inch and fold my arms across my chest. My heart thumps against my hand. He reaches for me and our bodies mesh as he wraps his arms around me. "What's wrong?"

I exhale sharply. "I...just don't want to get my hopes up, you know." He frowns, and that's when I realize my mistake. "I'm not saying you're going to bail before the thirty days. I'm not saying that at all."

"What are you saying?"

"I just...what if after thirty days my father still doesn't think I'm worthy of my trust fund? That I'm going to blow through it, or that investing it into a restaurant is a mistake?"

His brow furrows and his eyes hold a measure of sadness when he says, "I'm worried about that too, Kins."

I blink, a little surprised by that. "You are?"

"I've met your father."

I nod. "Yeah..."

"You want to do good things with it. You're responsible, and giving, and work harder than anyone I know. I don't know why he can't see that."

"He doesn't want to. He's punishing me for rebelling against what he wanted me to do with my life."

"It's your life, Kins. I hate that he dangles that trust fund like a carrot, so he can control you." His eyes search my face. "What if we found another way, a way where you don't have to feel indebted to him."

"I've been to the banks. I have zero collateral." I give a

very unlady-like snort. "My father certainly won't co-sign a loan."

"I figured as much." He sits on the small window ledge and pulls me between his legs. "Will you let me help you?"

My breath stalls. Is he suggesting what I think he's suggesting? I give a fast shake of my head. "Cason, no—"

"Hear me out."

I try to back up but he holds me to him, squeezing me with his legs as my hands disappear into his, his rough calluses scraping against the back of my fingers. "No, Cason. No. Never."

"You want to make it on your own. I get what you're saying. I also know how much you want to give back and help the community. This location is perfect for what you want to do, and I don't want to see you lose it. We can consider it a loan if you want, until you're in the black, but I am your husband so I'm not really sure how that will work," he says making light of the situation. I flick a glance over his shoulder to peer into the window. "Let's go in and you can think about it."

I nod, even though in my heart, I know I won't take him up on it. He's doing enough for me as it is. He opens the door, and waves to let me in first. My heart jumps into my throat as I examine the space, and the complete design for the restaurant comes to me in a flash. Before I can stop myself, excitement pumps through my blood.

"Oh, Cason, we can put the kitchen back there, there will be so much room, and think about all the tables we can have. I want it to be elegant, but homey, too, you know. I want it to be welcoming for everyone."

"I think it's perfect."

My hands go to my chest. "It is perfect. I can even do a booth here, by the window so customers can look out onto the street as they eat." My heart thumps, and I throw my arms around him. "Thanks for arranging this."

"I have a good feeling about it, Kins."

I squeal a little, letting the excitement pump through my veins. "This weekend, maybe I'll start drawing up what I want to do."

"Speaking of this weekend, we'd better hit the road if we want to make it there for the barbecue and bonfire."

We head back outside, and I give one last glance over my shoulder to memorize the space before Cason locks up. There's an extra spring in my step as we head back to the car, and I turn to look at Cason. My heart squeezes so tight in my chest, it brings tears to my eyes, and I quickly blink them back.

"Tacos for life," I tell him.

"For me?"

I squeeze his hand. "Yes, for you. For being so sweet."

"I just want to see you happy, Kins."

"Thanks, Cason, and don't worry. I won't tell anyone you're sweet."

He squeezes my hand back, and we climb into his car. I rest against the seat and close my eyes to envision my very own restaurant as he drives us to the grocery store for supplies for his cottage. Once we're loaded up with enough food to feed an army, we head to the beach. I sit up a little straighter when he pulls into the driveway, a gorgeous beach-side cottage rising up before us.

"This is yours?" I examine the beautiful two-story beach house, painted in seafoam green, with numerous plants in the window boxes. We had a cottage growing up, but barely spent any time there. Someday, if I work really hard and my restaurant is a success, I hope to have a place like this to go to.

"Yeah. Do you like it?"

"I love it. Did you plant those flowers?"

"No, I'm sure Alyssa did it. She knew you were coming and probably wanted to make it inviting. I'm not much of a green thumb."

I remember Alyssa from the wedding. We didn't get to talk much, but I found out she was a landscape artist in Vermont. Alek did a lot of traveling to see her, they still have a house there, but now that her grandmother passed away, she spends more time here in Seattle with Alek, aka, The Puck Charmer. I think it's so cute that the guys all have such fun names and I'm looking forward to getting to know the wives better.

"I don't get out here as often as I'd like, and when we're all here, the girls are always giving me a hard time about being alone. Guess they can't do it this time, can they?"

"Nope," I say and climb from the car. Children's laughter reaches my ears, as well as dogs barking. With the sun low on the horizon, I turn to take in the beach area and spot our friends in the distance. Jules and Rider have a place here, but I never made the time to come when they invited me. I was always pouring my heart, soul, and what little money I made back into my truck. With them off on their honeymoon, I won't see them this weekend, unfortunately.

"Want to go for a swim?" Cason asks, his mouth near my ear as he comes to stand behind me. He puts his arms around me, and I lean against him. I guess our friends know we're sleeping together. Heck, Cole caught us kissing on my truck. So there isn't much sense in avoiding public displays of affection.

Nina and the boys come running up to me, a big black dog following them. "Hey, Huxley," Cason says and falls on his butt when the dog practically leaps into his arms.

I laugh and the boys pile on top of their uncle. He carries on with them for a few minutes, and the sight pulls a smile from me. He's so good with his nephews. The man needs a family of his own. Want and need flood me as I picture myself in that happy family scenario.

"Okay, boys, let your uncle breathe." Nina picks the boys off, and they go running back to the water where everyone is playing. Nina leans in to give me a hug. "I'm glad you were able to come." She glances into the car. "How long are you guys planning on staying?" she asks when she sees all the food.

Luke comes sauntering over with a beer, and hands it to Cason. They click bottles and he takes a pull.

"Come on," Nina says and wraps her arm in mine. "Let's go have a glass of wine. My lazy brother can carry the groceries in and put them away."

"What's that Neaner-Nearner," he says and grabs her in a headlock. She jabs her elbow into his stomach and I laugh, loving the sibling rivalry. But then sadness envelopes me, wishing I had the same with my older sisters. I guess they figured if they freeze me out, I'd eventually fall in line and become the obedient daughter and go back to law school. I'm not even sure either one of them is happy. We all work long hours, but at least I enjoy what I'm doing.

She breaks free and gives him a punch to the gut. I chuckle, as she leads me away. "You two are pretty close," I say.

"Yeah, we are." She casts me a glance. "I never really understood how close we were until I was older." I frown, not really understanding what she means. "He's one of the good guys, Kins. I never knew how good until Cole and he filled me in on all the things my brother did for me when we were young."

"I don't understand." We follow a gravel path, leading to what I assume is her cottage. "What didn't you know?"

"Let's just say he's a guy of actions, not words."

"He said something like that to me actually. He said he always messes things up."

She nods, like she totally understands where he's coming from. "Probably because he does."

"He did something really sweet today, but do not tell him I said he was sweet," I say with a laugh as I glance over my shoulder to make sure he's not within ear shot.

"He does do a lot of sweet things. Like I said, he's a really great guy." We take the three steps leading to her place. "What great thing did he do?"

"He arranged for a viewing of the downtown space I want to rent. It was a really nice surprise."

"That's my brother, full of surprises."

"He even offered to help me with the rent until I get on my feet. He joked that it wasn't really helping since he's my husband," I say and do air quotes around that one word.

"Sounds like Cason, and it sounds like he's saying all the right things to you. That's a refreshing change. Wonder what that's all about." She pulls the door open and warm scents of vanilla and fresh baked apple pie reach my nostrils. That's when I remember Cason said they both did a lot of the cooking growing up.

"He's really good with your boys," I say.

"You're right, those kids love him, and my brother needs kids of his own. Now that you two are married...."

I roll my eyes. "You know it's just pretend. He's helping me out with a personal thing."

"Is that all that's going on?" she asks and I turn my head to examine the pictures on the wall, fearing she can read me as well as her brother. I study the family photos, love radiating from all the happy faces and wrapping around me. "You have a beautiful family"

"Thanks." She looks at me with big blue eyes that match her brother. "Do you want a family, Kinsley?"

I give a noncommittal shrug. "I know I say I'm anti-marriage..."

"You were hurt, I get it."

"But there is a part of me that wants all this, you know. How could I not? But I have to get my business off the ground and the thoughts of getting back out there dating." I fake a shiver. "It gives me a rash."

She laughs and loops her arm in mine again to lead me to the kitchen. "That I can understand. But you don't have to get back out there, you're married."

I roll my eyes because we both know it's a farce. She grabs a bottle of white wine from the fridge and holds it up. I nod. "Yes, please."

She pours two generous glasses and slides one across the kitchen island to me. I take a sip, and consider her brother, all the nice things he's done and said to me. "Can I ask you something?"

She tucks a curl behind her ear. "Sure."

"Has Cason ever been serious before?"

"No, not really. He dated my friend once, and I thought they might turn into more, but they didn't. After that, he came up with some two-week rule. I'm assuming you know all about that."

"Yeah, he actually mentioned it to me."

She frowns. "He did?"

"He just wanted to let me know not to expect more." I laugh to make light of it. "Not that I ever would."

"Is that right, Kinsley?" she asks like she can see right through me.

"That's right."

It's a lie. A great big, stupid, fat lie, and maybe coming here really was a bad idea.

CASON

"Who wants to go fishing in the morning?" Cole asks, and all the kids jump up and down. Well, everyone except Daisy—Zander and Sam's daughter.

"Eww, I am not touching a worm," Daisy says. I laugh. Daisy might be eight, but she's going on sixteen and her Mom and Dad are going to have their hands full when she really does hit her teen years. I glance at all the kids, and there's an odd little ache in my heart. Do I want this? Fuck yeah, I do. I want it. I want all of this with the sweet girl beside me. Maybe I have to convince her she does, too—and try not to fuck it up, by giving her what she needs emotionally, and not saying the wrong goddamn thing.

"What about you Kinsley, do you want to go fishing?"

"I'm with Daisy," Kinsley says, as Daisy pulls her marshmallow from the fire. The little girl steps up to Kinsley and offers her the gooey treat.

"Thank you," she says as she pulls it off.

"Mommy," Daisy says. "Tomorrow can we make my hair pink?"

Kinsley's gaze flies to Samantha's, like she's actually worried her free nature might cause conflict between mother and daughter.

Samantha shrugs. "Sure, why not. It's summer vacation. We can do something fun."

Daisy claps and grabs another marshmallow, as Kinsley smiles at Samantha. The two don't know each other well. They only recently met at the wedding. Zander and Sam live in Boston, but fly out to their summer cottage here every chance they get.

"We can have a girl's day," Katee says, and scoops up her tired little girl, Khloe. "But right now, I need to get this little one to bed." Luke jumps up and we all say goodnight as they saunter off.

"I want to stay at uncle Cason's tonight," Brandon says, and Cole jumps up.

"Maybe tomorrow night. It's their first night here and they are probably tired. Need a good night's sleep with no kids jumping on them at the crack of dawn to wake them." He shakes his head. "Wait, what am I saying?"

I laugh. "Tomorrow night, Brandon. You and Casey can stay over." I turn to look at Kinsley. "Are you okay with that?"

"Of course. I'd love to get to know my nephews better," she jokes. Even though right now they really are her nephews. "I grew up with all sisters. A house full of boys will be a refreshing break."

Cole and I both laugh at that. "Poor girl doesn't know what she's up against," Cole says, and I shake my head.

"In for a rude awakening," I agree.

"It can't be that bad, can it?" she asks and crinkles her nose.

"I'll leave you to answer that," Cole says. "Come on boys. You have to get up early for fishing, so let's move it."

"Are you coming?" Brandon asks me, and I glance at Kinsley. Honestly, I don't want to smother her this weekend, but I do want to spend as much time with her as possible. Does she want that, too? Want to make every minute together count?

"Go ahead," she says with a wave. "I plan to sleep in and then hang out with the girls."

Guess not.

"Okay, kiddo, I'll come," I say and inject a lightness into my voice that I don't feel. "Someone has to teach you how to properly cast, anyway. I can't remember the last time your dad caught anything at the lake, other than a cold."

"Why would I need your help when I have Alyssa?" Brandon says innocently enough, and Cole and Nina burst out laughing. So does Alyssa, who is in the process of stuffing a marshmallow between two chocolate cookies.

"Schooled," Nina says. She gives Brandon a high five even though he's completely confused by our reactions.

"Alyssa fishes?" Kinsley asks.

"She's amazing," I tell her. "Her grandfather had a rod in her hand by the time she was two. She out-fishes us all the time."

Casey rubs his eyes and lets loose a big yawn. "Okay boys, let's get going," Nina says.

"I'm not tired," Casey says, his eyeballs practically falling out of his head.

"Yeah, I can tell," Cole says and scoops him up.

"I don't want to go to bed," he whines.

"Casey," I say. "If you get a good night's sleep, we can get pancakes at your favorite restaurant for breakfast."

Casey smiles at me. "And a toy?"

"Of course. What are pancakes without a toy?" I say. Hand on her hips, Nina glares at me and I grin. "What?" I chuckle at the way her lips are twisted.

She points a finger at me. "Bribery on your part makes it harder for me to parent."

"It worked, didn't it? Look at Casey, he's ready for bed. Aren't you buddy?" Casey nods his head emphatically and I give him the thumbs up.

"Fine then, when you have your own kids, get ready for their aunt to bribe them. Then you'll see what it's like."

"Not going to happen little sister," I say, as an invisible band tightens around my heart, wanting that so badly.

"You're quite the negotiator," Kinsley says and leans into me.

"He's good at getting what he wants," Cole says with a smirk, and I toss a marshmallow at him, knowing full well he's talking about my rotating bedroom door—all the relationships I messed up. Why did I always say the wrong thing?

Because none of them were what you really wanted.

My entire body stiffens at that sudden epiphany. Holy shit, have I purposely been fucking up, sabotaging, saying the wrong thing, and keeping myself emotionally closed because while I want what my friends and sister have, I just never found the girl I wanted to have it with? As that rattles around in my brain, everyone gets up to get their kids off to bed, leaving Kinsley and me alone by the dying fire. I put my arm around her and breathe in her scent as she lays her head on my shoulder.

"I love all your friends, Cason. You have an amazing tribe."

"They're your friends, too."

"I only really know you guys through Jules and my food truck. It's nice getting to know everyone better."

"Just stay away from Liam. I don't like the way he's been looking at you."

She laughs and whacks my stomach. "Liam is a pussycat. Besides, he was into Emily, not me. Just like you," she says with a smile that does not reach her eyes. My stomach coils. What can I say to that? She's right, I was going after Emily, but what I found instead was so much better. I'm about to open my mouth and tell her that, when she lets loose a big sigh.

"It's so peaceful here," she says as I coil a long strand of her hair around my fingers. "So different from the city. A girl could get used to this."

"We can come here whenever you want."

"That's a nice offer, Cason, but soon enough you'll be back to practice and on the road. I'll be working on opening a new restaurant, and things will go back to normal between us."

I open my mouth wanting to ask for more, but what if I scare her off? Maybe instead of telling her, I need to show her what she means to me.

"It's nice to live in a fantasy every now and then, though."

"Yeah, it's nice," I say at the reminder of our timeline. That's still not going to stop me from doing my best to convince her we should make a go at this. Like she says, I'm quite the negotiator, and if there's one thing I know, actions speak louder than words.

She lifts her face to mine, and my God, my heart does a little flip. Her smile pulls me in and not even the toughest Seattle Shooter's defensive player could keep me from her. I press my lips to hers, and she tastes like sweet marshmallow and everything nice...everything I want.

Our lips linger, and our breathing is in sync as we exchange tender kisses without a care who's watching. The last embers of the fire flicker, and water laps gently against the shore.

"We never did go for that swim," I say. I jumped in earlier with the kids, and I'm still in my swim shorts.

"You want to go in?"

"I have an idea." I wag my brows at her. "See that wharf out there?"

She lifts her head and peers into the night to take in the wharf lit under the near full moon.

"Let me guess. You want to race to it, winner takes all?" she asks, as she pushes to her feet. She starts running, tugging her top off to reveal her bathing suit underneath. I jump up and go after her, tripping on my laces as I try to get my damn shoes off. She tugs on her shorts, and nearly falls into the sand as she tries to run, and by the time I reach her, my shoes and shirt gone, I'm laughing so hard I can hardly breathe.

"You're going to kill yourself." I put my arms around her and spin her.

"No, I'm going to beat you. I was on the swim team in high school."

"We'll see about that," I say and set her behind me.

"No fair. You're a cheater," she calls out as I wade out. She finishes undressing, and I nearly bite off my tongue when I find her in a bikini that showcases all her beautiful curves. My dick instantly hardens, despite the cold water. She splashes in after me, and I stand there too busy admiring her to realize she's been closing that gap.

She dives in when she reaches her waist and I lose her as she goes underwater. I dive in after her, and when I come up, I spot her ahead of me, just inches from the wharf. I push harder, and when I lift my head again, she's standing on the wharf doing a victory dance.

"Smart ass," I say and she turns and shakes her backside at me.

"Such a sore loser."

"Such an obnoxious winner," I tease.

She crooks her fingers. "That's right I'm the winner, now get your ass up here."

I hoist myself up, and stand next to her, and she steps into me, her hands going around my shoulders, our bodies meshed. Her lips find mine for a slow, simmering kiss, and I groan into her mouth.

"Think anyone can see us out here?" she asks.

"There you go again. Thinking about sex," I tease as my hard cock presses into her stomach.

She laughs. "You know I've never had sex outside, or under the stars before," she tells me. "Have you?"

"Can I plead the fifth?"

She laughs. "Sure but that answers my question." She goes quiet and then asks, "Is there anything we can do that you've not done with another woman? Something special?"

"You want to be my first for something?"

"Yes."

I get that she wants something special, especially after her douche bag ex telling her she was anything but, but everything about this woman is special. I keep trying to prove it, yet she's not seeing it.

"We got married, Kins. I'm your first husband and you're my first wife. That's pretty special."

She laughs. "It's not real, and I want something real, that's a first for both of us, you know. Something we can remember...later, when we're done. But I'm not sure that's possible." She laughs. "You do have a reputation." She runs her nails over my back lightly, and my body quivers. "Cold?" she asks.

"Hot, baby, for you." I make a move to kiss her and she pushes me off her. I stand there stunned. Was it something I said?

"I won," she reminds me, going into playful mode. "So..." She taps her chin like she's thinking about her prize.

"What do you want, Kinsley?" I ask, taking a step closer. Her breathing is deep, heavy, her gorgeous breasts rising and falling as desire races through her.

She looks down and her voice is soft, low, when she says, "I don't think it's something I should ask for."

My heart leaps. Jesus is she looking for more? Too afraid to ask since we set the terms for this 'marriage'?

She puts her hand on my chest. "Tell me," I say, in a soft voice, as I touch her chin and lift her eyes to mine.

"Have you ever had sex without a condom?" she asks quietly, like she's afraid someone might overhear us.

"No," I say, lowering my voice to match hers. "Have you?"

"Actually, yeah. I was in a long-term relationship and was on the pill."

"Are you still on it?" I ask, as the idea grips my balls and squeezes tight.

"Yes."

I lightly run my knuckles over her face. "I'm clean Kinsley. I promise you that."

"I believe you. I'm clean, too. Like squeaky clean. I haven't been with anyone since 'he who shall not be named' broke it off with me. Well, until you came along."

"I like that you broke your dry spell with me."

She makes a sound. "Yeah, but that was kind of a mistake, Cason."

"Yeah, it was a mistake—.

She cuts me off and says, "Do you want to have sex without a condom?"

My dick jumps in my pants. I always wrap, and the idea of skin on skin with this beautiful woman...well, I might just lose my fucking mind.

"It won't really be anything special. I've done it before," she adds.

"It'll be special." I take a deep breath and exhale harshly. "Believe me, it'll be real fucking special."

The next thing I know, she's dipping her hand into my shorts, and taking my cock in her palm. I laugh, and she looks up at me. "Am I not doing this right?"

"Oh, baby you're doing it right. I was just thinking, we

would have been doing it without a condom out here anyway because I don't have one in my swim shorts."

"But there were always other things we could do. We can't take the chance of getting pregnant."

"No, I would have taken the risk," I say. "That's how much I need to be inside you."

She smiles, like she enjoys the power she has over me, the way I forget all about the real world, and the consequences of our actions when I'm with her.

"Well I would have kept my wits and put a stop to it," she says.

"Really. Let's see about that," I say. I slide my hand around her wet body, and pull her tight against me. A fine shiver goes through her and my lips close over hers for a hot, heavy, passion-filled kiss that I hope, leaves her a little dizzy. Our tongues tangle and play and her moans of pleasure curl around me.

I break the kiss, and find that sensitive spot on her neck until she's writhing in need. She lifts one leg, and rubs up against me as she wraps it around me, and I bite back a smile as I take her to that place where common sense is a thing of the past. She's the only woman in the world who's ever taken me there, and that's a first.

I sink to my knees and pull her down with me. I lower her to her back, and she reaches for me. I climb over her. "Look up," I say, and she does.

"So beautiful." Her voice is a soft, drowsy whisper, that wraps around my soul.

"Not as beautiful as what I'm looking at," I say, and she turns her focus back to me.

"There are times you really do say all the right things, Cason."

I tug her bathing suit top down to expose her pert nipples, realizing that with her, it's easy to say the right things. "I'm only telling the truth, though," I say. With her it's easy to say what's in my heart, because I like her so much, and truly want this to work.

"If I told you I wanted my mouth on your gorgeous pussy, would those be the right words?" I tease as I shimmy lower, pressing kisses to her hot flesh.

"The absolute best words," she says, tossing her head from side to side. Her hips come up and her sweet honeyed scent fills my senses. My God, I am going to eat this woman until she's crying out my name and begging for more. I have never wanted to pleasure a woman as much as I do with her.

I position myself between her legs, and slide her bikini bottoms down. I set them aside carefully. I do not want her running back to our cottage naked, everyone seeing what's mine.

What's mine?

Fuck yeah, she's mine. She's all mine. She's Mrs. Kinsley Elizabeth Palmer-Callaghan. My wife. Now I just have to convince her that a relationship is not a bad thing and that I'm not going to hurt her like her ex. Then maybe we can have a chance at this thing called a future. I part her legs, and run my hands up her thighs, groaning as the heat of her sex reaches my fingertips.

"You're burning up," I say.

"Uh huh," is all she says in response and I resist a chuckle. Oh, yeah, she would have kept her wits about her my ass. But Goddammit, I love this. I love the way she opens up under my touch, sheds all inhibition and just takes what she wants without any insecurities. Sure I made other women moan, sure I was adamant that I pleasured them properly first, but this woman's pleasure is more important to me than breathing. I want her to know she has value, and show her that she deserves to be worshipped. She was just never with the right man, much like I was never with the right woman.

I lick her sweet cunt, all the way from the bottom to the top, flattening my tongue to press it against her swollen clit. I steal a quick glance up, and her eyes have fallen shut.

"Open your eyes, baby. Look at the stars."

"I don't need them open to see stars," she says and I chuckle against her sex, which illicits a moan as the vibrations go through her body.

"Open them anyway. I want you to see those stars as I take you into space." Her lids lift, and I lick her some more, knowing her body well now. Know how to take her higher and higher and leave her lingering.

I put a finger inside her, and her walls clamp around me. She's chanting my name, and my heart beats that much faster. I finger fuck her the way she likes, and circle her clit with the soft blade of my tongue. I slide a second finger into her and a whimpering sound reaches my ears. Jesus, she is so close. I inch out, and her gaze flies to mine.

"Cason," she says, her breath so ragged I can barely make out my name on her lips.

"Do you have your wits about you Kinsley?"

"God, no. Please put your cock inside me." I chuckle, but who am I to fucking talk? I can barely remember my own name as her need wraps around my cock and strokes hard.

My chuckle dies an abrupt death and morphs into a heated moan. "Kins."

"I want to feel your thickness inside me. I want to come all over your big cock."

Holy fuck, yes. It takes all my effort to find the words to ask, "If you weren't on the pill would you still be saying that?"

"Yes." She grabs my shoulders. "You win. I want you so much, I don't care about anything but your cock inside me."

"I win because I'm here with you, Kins. But you're about to win, too. You did after all, beat me to the dock, so I think you should come all over my face, and then again with my cock inside you."

"Yes, Cason. All...the...right...words."

I dip into her, changing the rhythm and pace, plunging deep and fast, and hard, circling the bundle of nerves inside as I take her clit into my mouth. Within seconds she's bursting all over my tongue, and crying out my name. Her fingers go to my hair and she tugs as she rides out the waves. I lick her, eat her, bury my face deep as her liquid desire soaks me. I come up for air and her eyes are dark, intense, and locked on mine. I don't think I've ever seen such need on her face. I'm not going to make her wait one more second. I'm going to fulfil that need, now.

"My cock. Inside you." It's all I can say. Creating full, coherent sentences is a thing of the past and I'm okay with it. I lay over her and she opens her legs, welcoming my unsheathed cock into her tight body. In one thrust I'm high inside, and her muscles squeeze me so tight, I'm pretty much a goner. How the fuck does sex with her get better and better every time?

Oh, probably because I like her in a way I've never liked another. She's been hurt in the past, is relationship shy, so I need to tread carefully, keep my feelings to myself. Which is utterly fucking insane. I'm the guy who can never express his feelings properly and the one time I want to, the one time I want to jump up and scream to anyone who will listen that this woman is stealing my heart, I can't.

How's that for fucked up?

14

KINSLEY

After waking up to soft kisses from Cason, I fell back to sleep as he joined the others for a friends and family fishing trip. I much prefer a comfy bed over bugs and worms. Now it is late morning and the sound of the water lapping against the shore and the birds chirping nearby, pull me wide awake. I stretch out, my body sore in the most glorious ways. Forcing my legs to move, I dash to the bathroom for a quick shower, not really wanting to sleep away any more moments of this trip.

I wash thoroughly, touching my body and reminiscing about all the ways Cason made love to me last night. Made love? I'm not sure I can call it that, but his touch, the way he talked to me, wrapped around my heart and hugged. Everything about last night was beautiful, and touching, and not something I'm ready to quit. I don't even want to think about how many days we have left, and that's just not good.

Once washed, I dry, tug on my bathing suit, and grab my cover-up. I wander slowly through the cottage. Has Cason ever brought any other women here? Has he made love to them in the very same bed I just crawled out of? Ribbons of unease curl around my stomach and twist. Honestly, it shouldn't bother me if he has. I mean he is known for his reputation, and heck, what we have isn't special. We can't even find one thing to do that we haven't already done with someone else. Is it stupid that I asked about that? Probably, and I hate that it bothers me so much. The truth is, every time he touches me, looks at me and worships my body, he makes me feel special. Deep down, though, I'm smart enough to know I'm not.

Then again, maybe I am.

My ex's words hurt, left me insecure, and while I like to think I'm over it, a confident woman, maybe all that uncertainty is lingering just below the surface, holding me back from telling the man how I feel about him. I work to push my worry and uncertainty down as I glance at the photos on the wall. I can't help but smile, and maybe fall for him just a little tiny bit more. Is that even possible? I touch the frame of one picture to straighten it. Cason doesn't seem like the kind of guy to hang photos of his childhood or his nephews. I can only assume Nina was behind this, trying to make his house a home.

If I lived here—.

I quickly cut off those thoughts. I can't go there. We're just pretending right? Or are we? My God, I am just so confused about everything. If I wasn't so darn worried about messing things up and scaring him off, I'd come right out and ask.

I tug on my bathing suit cover-up and make my way downstairs to find Nina and Katee knocking on the front door of the cottage. "Good morning," I say and swing it open. Sunshine and a warm summer breeze wash over me and help lighten my insides. This weekend is about having fun, not worrying over my future, so I'm going to shut down all those worrisome thoughts and do just that.

"You just getting up?" Katee asks as she adjusts her daughter Khloe in her arms.

"Yeah, late night." I widen the door even more and wave them in, hoping they can't see the blush crawling up my neck as I think about the reason I was up until the crack of dawn. "I need coffee."

"I could use a cup," Nina says. Katee steps in, and Nina closes the door behind them. She spreads her arms and takes a deep breath. "I love my boys, but my God it's nice to be child-free for a few hours."

Katee and I laugh at that, and she bounces her daughter. "I'm hoping when little missus here gets older, she'll enjoy tagging along with the others."

Nina looks past my shoulders, her gaze landing on a picture of her, Cason, and Cole, probably taken around ten years ago. She smiles, and it's easy to tell her thoughts are a million miles away. "Cason took me everywhere with him," she says.

"Really. I didn't know that." I start down the hall, and the women follow.

"He was a great big brother. I always thought I was a nuisance, but he liked having me around, even though he never came right out and said it." A pause and then she continues with, "Is he still saying all the right things to you, Kinsley?" I steal a glance at her over my shoulder and note her curious grin.

"Ah, yeah, kind of. Let's get that coffee going." We make our way into the kitchen and I go straight for the coffee pot, needing the caffeine to wake me up. "Did you decorate this place?" I ask.

"I had a little help from my friends."

"I love all the pictures. It's so homey." I bite my lip, wanting to ask more, wanting to ask how many women he's brought here, but I don't want anyone getting the wrong idea.

"The place would be all bare walls if he had it his way. It needed a woman's touch, and since he's never brought a woman here, I had no choice but to do it myself. I'm glad you like it."

My heart leaps at that little tidbit of information. As Nina eyes me, I try not to show any outward reaction, but I don't think I'm pulling off casual by any means. The small smile on her face as she takes me in speaks volumes. I'm transparent. I didn't even have to ask the question for her to know it was lingering on my tongue, dancing in my eyes.

Making herself at home, and really, it's more Nina's home than mine, she pulls the milk from the fridge. She looks at all the food before closing the door. "How much food did you bring?" she asks.

I laugh and open the cupboards until I find the mugs. I set three on the counter. "I thought it would be fun if I cooked for everyone tonight."

"Sweetie," Katee says. "You do enough cooking for us on your truck. Let us take care of you. Better yet, let the guys take care of us all," she adds with a chuckle. "We deserve the break for all we put up with. Isn't that right, Khloe?" she says to her toddler.

Katee might be complaining, but she's doing it playfully. The warm smile on her face, and the adoration shining in her eyes is a good indication of how much she loves her family, and I get the sense it's very give and take between husband and wife. I like that in a relationship. Friends and partners. Taking care of one another. Through good times and bad. In the bad times my ex tossed me to the curb. I can't ever imagine Cason doing something like that. My heart does an odd little flip in my chest, and I clear my throat to pull myself together when I catch the way the two women are staring at me as I go all dreamy like over my crush.

"I love cooking," I say, getting back on topic. "Tonight I

thought I'd do homemade flatbread pizzas. I wanted to keep the kids in mind, so I'm sure it's cheese and pepperoni for them. The adult versions will be a little fancier with grilled chicken and pineapple salsa."

"Get in my belly," Nina says with a grin.

I smile back, happy that she likes my choice. "It's good practice for when I finally get my own restaurant, too."

Katee's eyes go big. "Ohmigod, that is so exciting. I do love your tacos though. Tell me you'll still be making them."

"I will be, but I want to expand, use more locally sourced food, and find more ways to help those less fortunate in our community."

"I love the pay-it-forward program you have on your truck," Katee says.

"Okay, that's it," Nina says and presses her palms to the table. "I love my brother but you're far too good for him. I'm sure Mom and Dad would agree."

I laugh a bit uneasily and say, "Thanks."

"You're really not going to meet them?" she asks, and I don't get the confusion on her face. We explained that we were doing this for my situation, and it was best not to involve his parents.

I shake my head firmly. "No." Wanting to change the subject I redirect by saying, "Thank you both for all your contribution to the pay-it-forward program. Cason has some really awesome people in his life."

"We're in your life, too," Nina says, like once we get our marriage annulled, I'll still be in their circle, and coming to their bonfire events at the beach. My heart sits heavy at that, but I keep it to myself.

Speaking of events...

"So uh, I have a favor to ask." The coffee pot beeps and I fill our cups. Both sets of eyes are trained on me as I hand them their cups. I sit at the table and say, "My parents want to throw a wedding party for Cason and me since they weren't invited to the actual..." I pause to do air quotes around the word "wedding." "It will be big and elaborate and I'll hate every second of it." Nina takes a sip of her coffee and her lips twist, but it's not because the coffee is bitter. "You don't have to if you don't want to," I say quickly when I read her body language. Oh, God, have I gone too far, asked too much?

"Of course, I want to," she says. "We'd do anything for you. You're family. But do you think it's a good idea to throw an elaborate party, when you two are going to get your marriage...annulled?"

"No actually, I don't."

"That settles it then," she says quickly, the smile on her face and the lift of her chin suggesting she's very proud of herself. "There will be no annulment."

I give her a look that suggests she might have just lost her mind. "I can't stay married, just because I think a party for a 'fake' marriage is a bad idea."

"Stay married because it's what you want then," Katee says and tugs on one of her daughter's braids to play with her. "And enjoy the party. You both deserve that."

"Wait, it's not..." With all this coming at me fast, my thoughts begin to spin around in my already rattled brain. "I'm saying there shouldn't be a party. I don't even want one. But my parents are insisting. God knows they can't have my sudden Vegas wedding look bad on them." I frown and look down. "Cason was kind enough to agree."

"You need this marriage because of your parents?" Nina asks gently.

"Fake marriage," I correct. "Well, technically it's real, and I'm not lying, but it feels like I am, you know."

"You're not lying. You guys really did get married," Katee

says. She grins. "And from the happy look on both yours and Cason's face, it's really agreeing with you."

"We've been having fun, sure, but maybe what we're doing is wrong—"

"Marriage is never wrong when two people care for each other, Kinsley. You guys just jumped into it sooner rather than later," Nina says, and Katee nods in agreement.

"Wait, what." My hair hits my face as I shake my head so hard, I nearly give myself a concussion. "No, you guys have it all wrong. This isn't something we planned to do later. It was a mistake. Like a colossal mistake."

God, I wish it wasn't.

I lift my head when I hear a noise and spot Cason coming into the kitchen. He puts on a smile but there's a sag in his shoulders that doesn't go unnoticed by me. Did he just hear me say marriage isn't something we planned to do later? That it was a colossal mistake? If so, why would that make him sad? He's told me where he stands, agreed that it was a mistake, just like him falling into my bed that night was a mistake. He thought he was sleeping with Emily for God's sake.

"You're back early. What's the matter?" Nina asks. "Alyssa putting you guys all to shame?"

"Funny, Neaner-Nearner." He casts me a quick glance. "The flies are starting to get bad and we're low on bug spray. I volunteered to come back and get it. Cole said you guys have some," he says and looks at Nina.

"Then what are you doing over here?" she asks with a smug grin. "Why aren't you at my house getting it?" She winks at him. "Oh, wait, I know why. You came back here for a quickie."

He rolls his eyes at his sister, but it lightens the tension inside me. "First, you're here, aren't you? Maybe I checked your place and couldn't find you. Second, I am not talking about my sex life with my little sister, or anyone else."

"Come on Katee, I think that's our cue to exit." They both stand up, and Cason gives little Khloe's fingers a kiss as she reaches for him. It's so goddamn adorable, air seizes in my lungs, and love fills my heart. "Come and get it when you're done doing whatever it is you're over here for."

"Go," Cason says, his gaze trained on me.

She blinks, and teasing like the younger sister she is, she says, "So I'll see you in about five minutes then?"

He shakes his head and Nina and Katee's laughter follow them out the door. Once we're alone, I say, "Did you check her place?"

"No."

"So, the quickie—" I say, reminding myself that maybe I shouldn't get my hopes up, that maybe this is all about tacos and sex. God, what am I saying? It has to be. If it meant more, he'd want to introduce me to his parents, right?

"I wasn't coming here for a quickie. I mean it's not that I don't want one, or want to be inside you every chance I get, but I just wanted to see you, make sure you got enough sleep after me keeping you up all night, and to make sure your morning was going well."

My heart leaps in my chest. My God, he really is the sweetest man on the planet.

"Marriage is never wrong when two people care for each other, Kinsley."

Nina's words bounce around inside my head as Cason brushes his knuckles over my cheeks. Could she be right? Could Cason really care about me? Yes, I know he *cares* about me. He wouldn't be doing all this if he didn't. The man cares about everyone. He'd walk on fire for his family and friends, but that does not mean what's between us is...love. Right?

Right.

"I'm good," I say around the lump in my throat. "I fell

back to sleep no problem, and it was nice to wake up to company."

He angles his head like he's not sure he believes me. "Those two weren't giving you a hard time, were they?"

I laugh. "No, I love them. They are awesome." I go up on my toes and brush my lips over his. "You're the only one who gives me a hard time," I say and rub my pelvis against his thickening cock.

He groans and it vibrates through me. "Keep that up and this really will turn into a quickie."

"I don't mind," I say. "But what about the spray for the guys? Aren't they waiting on it?"

"Yeah, but they have enough for the kids," he says and follows it up with a devious snort. "As far as the guys, screw them. Let them get eaten alive."

"Oh?"

His hands span my ribcage, his thumbs lightly brushing my nipples through my cover-up and bikini top. My lids turn heavy as desire pulls at me. As they fall shut, a little moan catches in my throat and I arc into his touch, let him know how much I welcome it, how much I don't want him to stop.

"They've been giving me a hard time," he says. My lids open, surprised, and I take in the darkening of his blue eyes as anger and desire mingle.

"Why?" I ask, in a breathless whisper.

"Insinuating that I won't make it past two weeks." He pushes his cock against me, and I grow wet between my legs. It's crazy how much I want him again. "They're getting on my fucking nerves about it, too."

"It kind of is your record, Cason," I say and put my hands under his T-shirt. His muscles quiver beneath my touch, and I love the way he reacts. I scrape my nails over him gently and lean in to take in his scent. It trickles through my blood, and arouses me even more.

"Yeah, but this time I have a very good reason for lasting longer," he murmurs, as he dips his head, his lips so close to mine, I can almost taste him.

"Sex and tacos," I say, hoping, praying he tells me it's more than that.

"Something like that," is all he says and my heart tightens in my chest. God, I am so confused about us. I give myself a fast, hard lecture and remind myself that while I'm here, I'm not going to worry about the future; I'm simply going to bask in the now, and the way this man touches me. If he walks away with my heart in his palm after two weeks, or a month, I'll deal with it then.

"Okay, since we're on the topic of hard times and getting eaten alive," I say and back up, until I'm practically sitting on the kitchen table.

"What are you getting at?" he growls.

I peel my cover-up off, and I'm instantly rewarded with a heated moan. I point to his pants. "Take them down, just a bit. I want you fully dressed for this quickie."

"You're full of surprises, Kinsley. I like it," he says as he tears into his jeans. "I like it a lot."

"Let's see if you like this," I say and spin around, bending myself over the table and putting my ass in the air.

"Jesus, fuck," he says and comes up behind me. He grips my hips, rubs his cock over my ass. "You're killing me, Kins."

He sinks to the floor, and grips my bikini bottoms, lowering them only to my knees. His hot breath feathers over my naked flesh, and he slides a hand between my thighs, which I can hardly spread, not with my bikini bottoms keeping me restrained.

He slides a thick finger into me. "Jesus, you are so wet." He parts my lips, and his tongue is on me, licking and entering me, eating at me like a man starved. I quake against the table, my nipples so hard, I'm sure I'm going to scar the wood.

"Fuck me, Cason," I say and he climbs to his feet. The sound of him working his hand over his cock thrills me and before I know it, he's at my opening, thrusting into me, hard and deep, and filling me to the hilt. "God, yes."

He grunts and grips my hips, and I know I'll have little finger bruises to commemorate this quickie. I love the idea of that. He groans and thrusts, then continues pounding on my cervix, taking me higher and higher. Our sex is hot and hard, neither of us exhibiting finesse. We're both acting on baser instincts, chasing the same goal of giving and taking pleasure. It's raw. It's blunt. It's so goddamn perfect tears form in my eyes.

My entire body tightens as the physical and emotional tangle, and the second he slides a hand between my legs, I come all over his big, fat cock. As I explode around him, he presses kisses to my neck and back. His hands loosen on my hips, his touch a bit gentler as he pushes deep and stills high inside me. He lets go, fills me with his hot cum, and I close my eyes as my body and heart absorb this man.

"Cason," I murmur. "I...I..." I have no idea what it is I want to say, all I know is that the emotions are washing over me like a damn tsunami and hot tears are threatening to spill, but not because I'm sad. I've never been happier, never been touched so deeply in all my life—who would have thought a quickie would affect me like this.

"I know, Kins. I know," is all he says as he wraps his arms around me, and lifts me from the table until my back presses against his chest. His heart pounds against my body, as he links his hands at my stomach, holding me to him. His embrace is so tender and loving, my knees nearly give—in fact, they do—but he's right there to hold me.

His breathing is harsh against my neck, warm and wet,

and wonderful. How can a man touch me like this if he didn't have deeper feelings? Or is that just wishful thinking on my part?

He slowly pulls out of me, and I instantly miss his warmth. He disappears for a split second, and before I can even turn to see where he's gone, he's back, putting a tissue between my legs to clean me. I quiver, and his soft chuckle makes me laugh.

"Is this turning you on?" he asks, his mouth near my ear.

"Like you said, all I think about is sex."

"Lucky me." He inches back and groans. "Shit."

"What?" I ask.

"Please tell me that was at least five minutes or I'm never going to hear the end of it from Nina."

"I'm pretty sure it wasn't."

"Great. She is never going to let this go."

I blink innocently. "There is a solution, Cason."

"Yeah?"

I put my hands over his and hug him to me, not wanting him to rush off. "We could always do it again. Add a minute or two."

He sinks his teeth into my flesh. "You're going to pay for that."

15

CASON

I can't stop smiling. Sure, I look like a damn idiot, but being here with Kinsley, the insane sex we had earlier this morning, her bent over the kitchen table offering herself up to me, was like icing on the cake and absolutely blew my fucking mind. How the hell did I get so lucky? Oh, I know. Because I made a mistake one night in Vegas. Best goddamn mistake of my life, that is.

As I look at her now, dressed in denim shorts and a snug T-shirt coming from the cottage with a tray of flatbread pizzas for the kids, my heart thunders. She grins at me, and it's enough to steal the oxygen from my lungs.

One thing is for certain, even though we set the rules, over the last week, I became invested in her, in more ways than one. She's everything and then some and I think the longer we're together, the better and better I get at expressing myself. The opposite of every other girl I've been with and if that doesn't tell me something, nothing will.

"Pizza, pizza, pizza," the kids all chant and they pound their hands on the large picnic table. Well, everyone except Casey who is too busy drinking a sugary soda, something

Nina doesn't normally let him have. But I'm guessing she's getting him all hyped up for me tonight. I'm on to her scheme, but I don't care. I'm looking forward to hanging with the boys, and Kinsley seems on board, too, which means I plan to let them stay up late and sleep in.

I glance at Daisy, who gives Kinsley a huge smile as Kins slides a flatbread onto her plate. Kinsley compliments Daisy on her bright pink hair, and the child beams in response. I love how Daisy wants to emulate her. Kinsley is a good role model. She's definitely going to be a great mother, once she moves beyond past hurts and opens herself up to love again.

Love?

Yeah, man. Love. That's exactly what I feel for this woman and pray to fucking God, she starts to feel that way about me. I'll do whatever it takes to gain her trust, show her that I'm not going to run away, because she's making her own choices, even if they don't mesh with my agenda. Compromise is what relationships are about, right? Alyssa and Alek did long-term in order to make it work.

"What are you grinning about, asshole?" Cole says as he hands me a beer.

"All your bug bites," I tell him and tip the bottle to my mouth. He shoves me and I nearly choke as I swallow. But maybe I deserve to be shoved. I did take my time getting back to the lake.

"Dude, you left us hanging. What kind of a team player are you?"

I give a casual shrug and dangle the bottle between my legs. "I had some things that needed taken care of. I told you that."

"Glad it only took five minutes." He smirks at me and I make a mental note to kill my sister. "Otherwise we would have been eaten alive."

"Fuck," I mumble and glance at Nina who is grinning at

me. I point to her in warning and she just saunters off to help Kinsley put the food in front of all the hungry kids.

"She fits right in," Cole says as he drops into a fold out chair beside me.

"Uh huh," I say as the warm summer breeze blowing in off the water rustles Kinsley's hair, and flutters around the T-shirt I plan to remove from her body later.

Cole waves his hand in front of my face and I whack it away. "Think I should be worried about losing my car?"

"Uh huh."

"What's this about losing your car?" Liam asks, coming up to us. He scratches his balls. "Oh, right. I remember." He points to Cole. "Your car," he stops to point to me. "Or you don't get laid for six months."

I glare at him. "Shut up, Liam. How the fuck does he know?" I ask Cole. Shit, if anyone else got wind of this, I can't imagine Kinsley would like it much. Or at all.

"He overheard on the phone the other night. He won't say anything. Right, Liam?"

Liam opens his mouth like he's about to say more, but someone on the beach, who happens to be in a tiny bikini, catches his attention, and he says, "Be right back."

"You like her, huh?" Cole says when we're alone.

"Uh huh."

"Enough to stick around for a whole month."

I slowly turn to him and grin as I hold my hand out, palm up. "Get ready to hand the keys over my friend."

"What happens after the month is over, when you've helped her out and she no longer needs you?" he asks.

My entire body stiffens, and the air in my lungs goes cold. Is that what's going to happen? When she no longer needs me, she's going to walk away? I can't let that happen. "Working on it."

He leans into me, his face serious. "Don't fuck this up."

His words hit like a slap and slam around my brain. Wait. Why *wouldn't* he want me to fuck it up? His car is on the line. He needs me to fuck it up. "I won't," I say adamantly, although there is a measure of unease racing through my veins.

"We'll see."

"I won't," I say again.

Before he can say anything, Kinsley comes over, but stops in her tracks when she sees the way Cole and I are glaring at one another. I consider him my brother. My closest friend in the whole world. I love him. We're ride and die buddies. Why the hell is he riding me like this? It's not like him. He smiles at me, letting me know we're okay, that he's just messing with me, and I soften.

"Did I interrupt something?" Kinsley asks.

"No, Cole was just about to go get something for all his bug bites," I say and a streak of pink crawls up Kinsley's neck as Cole shoves me. I burst out laughing as he makes his way to the cooler to grab another beer.

"Everything okay?" Kinsley asks.

"Fine. We were just having a discussion."

"Seemed serious." She glances over her shoulder. "Is he still giving you a hard time?"

"Yeah."

She makes a fist and slams it into her palm. "Want me to take care of that? I'm tougher than I look."

The tightness in my neck releases and I grab her, pull her to me until she's sitting on my lap. "So tough," I say and kiss her. One of the kids at the table makes an "eww" sound and we break apart. "Rain check?" I ask as she stands. Before she steps away, I tug her to me again. "You went through a lot of trouble preparing all this food today. That was really nice of you."

"Shh," she says and glances over her shoulder. "I'm a

badass, remember. Look at me with all these piercings. Don't say that too loud, I have a reputation to uphold."

"You're anything but a bad ass, although you do have a hell of an ass."

She chuckles. "A rebel?"

"You might seem like a rebel to your family, Kins," I say, going serious. Jesus, I'm still pissed at the way they treated her, dismissed what's important to her. I wish to hell she didn't have to take the money left by her grandfather. He would have wanted her to have it, yes, but in no way do I want her to feel indebted to her family—or to me. I want to do this for her, but she seems hell bent on doing it herself. "Everyone here adores you, even Daisy. You're an inspiration and a good example."

The smile she gives me wraps around my heart and squeezes tight. "You're sweet."

"Hush," I say and give her a whack on the ass. I glance over her shoulder. "I'm starving."

"Our pizzas are coming right out."

"Let me help you."

We head inside and the fresh scent of bread fills my senses. She pulls trays from the oven, and I shake my head. "Your restaurant is going to be a huge hit."

"Thank you." She gestures with a nod. "Grab the cutter and we'll slice these up."

We cut up the slices and carry them out. As the children eat at one picnic table, we all take the other.

"Kins, as much as I said you didn't need to cook for us, I'm sure glad you did," Katee says biting into the flatbread. "This is so good."

I put my hand on her thigh under the table and give it a squeeze.

"Since you spent all day making us food," I tell her. "I'll let you off the hook tonight. We don't have to take the boys."

"But I was looking forward to it. I have something very special planned," Kinsley says, and I eye her.

"Yeah?" I ask. "What is it?"

"It's kind of a surprise for you, too," she says softly as I refill her wine.

"Um, excuse me," Nina says holding out her glass. "Now that you have Kinsley, your sister doesn't matter?" she says with a smirk.

I reluctantly tear my gaze away and grumble as I fill my annoying sister's glass. Kinsley turns to Alyssa. "Sorry about all this," she says. "I didn't realize you'd be catching so many fish for us all."

A round of groans go around the table as Alyssa laughs. "What?" Kinsley's gaze goes around the table to take in my friends and family. "Was it something I said?" she asks so innocently, I'm not even sure she's teasing. "Oh, wait, I get it," she says. "You all think I'm pointing out that Alyssa caught all the fish, and you guys came home pathetically empty-handed."

I nudge her and she turns my way, a grin on her face. "Nice one," I say.

"We can do a fish fry tomorrow afternoon before we go back," Alyssa says.

"You guys want me to cook them?" She laughs when a round of yesses go around the table. "Is that a yes?" she asks, and I love how comfortable she is with us all, how easily she fits in. That's because she belongs here.

She belongs with me.

We all dig into our food and I savor the flavors. She arches a brow, like my opinion is important to her. "It's delicious, Kins. Best I've ever had."

"You're just saying that," she says and whacks me.

"Make no mistake about it. Your restaurant will be Seattle's hot spot within a week."

"Well I hope you're right, because I don't need any more mistakes in my life. I've made enough of them already," she says with a laugh and nudges me. "We all have."

My heart tightens a little. Does she not know that night was my best mistake? I make a mental note to tell her, when we're alone.

We continue to talk about nothing and everything until the food is gone and the sun is low on the horizon. After the meal, we all help clean up, all except Kinsley. I sent her to the adirondack chair with a glass of wine to sketch out her design for her restaurant, since she did all the work.

Once the dishes are done, it's dark, and since everyone is tired from an early morning, we all head back to our cottages. I go with my sister to help get the boys packed up for my place.

"You sure you don't mind?" Nina asks. "You didn't have anything personal planned for tonight?"

"No, we're good. Kinsley wants to do this, too."

"I like her, you know."

"Yeah, I know," I say as I take Casey's little hand in mine.

"I don't think I've ever seen you so happy before, big brother," she says and reaches up to rustle my hair. The boys laugh. "Don't let her get away, okay?" she says, her eyes and voice much more serious.

"I'm not sure—"

"She likes you, too, Cason. I've seen the way she looks at you."

My heart does some ridiculous cartwheel in my chest. "What's not to like?" I say giving her my best smart-assed comment, but deep inside I'm a hot mess of hope.

"Go," she says and points to the door. "And take that big ego with you." I open the door and she looks at the boys. "You guys be good for Uncle Cason and Aunt Kinsley, okay."

Aunt Kinsley.

Wow, weird. I never stopped to think that she was their aunt. Their only aunt. My throat tightens. Jesus, if she walks when this is over, I'm not going to be the only one dealing with loss. These boys are getting to know her, and they like her. I usually don't bring women into their lives. They do not need to see one coming and going all the time. That's just not fair.

But Kinsley is no ordinary woman. Is that why I allowed her into their lives, because deep down, right from the start, I thought maybe I wouldn't fuck things up, because this is something I really wanted?

We walk along the path, and the outside light is on as we approach my cottage. A little bubble of excitement wells up inside me and a smile I have no control over spreads across my face. I like the idea of her inside, waiting for me.

"Up you go," I say to Casey, as Brandon dashes up the stairs. "We're here," I say as we enter.

"In the kitchen," she calls out and we head down the hall. The second I enter the kitchen, see what's sitting on the kitchen table, the world sways around me.

"You have got to be kidding me!"

16

KINSLEY

My heart jumps into my throat as Cason stands there, completely still, his brow furrowed, his gaze going from my very old Easy Bake Oven, to me, back to the ancient toy again. His expression is a mix of astonishment and disbelief and my throat practically closes over as I see the pleasure dancing in his eyes.

"What's that thing?" Brandon asks, as he comes into the kitchen to examine the very strange looking oven from another generation. I'm not even sure they make something similar today.

"It's—" I begin, but stop when Cason talks.

"It's only the coolest toy in the world," he says. "And the best surprise I've ever received in my entire life."

His gaze lifts to mine, and my heart leaps into my tight throat as he gazes at me with pure adoration. "You did this for me?" he asks in a low voice, a storm brewing behind intense eyes.

"I thought it would be fun, you know. We can make some cakes or brownies." I reach behind me and pull out a full-size cake mix. "They don't make the little ones anymore, but we can use this," I say, holding up the big box of dark chocolate delight, a little frazzled by his reaction. I thought he'd get a kick out of it, but there is more going on beneath the surface.

"I can't believe you did this." He lets go of Casey's hand and the little boy saunters over, examining the machine like it's the eighth wonder of the world. That makes me laugh. Kids today are so hooked on video games they have no idea how much fun these old things were. Although, all the offspring of all the Seattle Shooters who are here this weekend aren't plunked in front of the television. No, they're outside playing and swimming and fishing. If I ever had kids, these are the ones I'd want them to be playing with.

My stomach takes that moment to squeeze. Yes. I want kids. I want them with the man who is staring at me with warmth and appreciation. The world closes in a little, the room growing smaller, as part of me thinks it's quite possible that I could have it all with this man, considering the way he's staring at me.

"Cason..." He blinks as if to take himself out of his trance, and a stupid measure of worry, thanks to past experiences, seeps under my skin. Did I make a mistake? Am I reading him wrong? Is this just silly? "Do you no—"

"I love it," he says, and I fold my arms around myself, loving that word on his tongue. "How...when? We traveled here together."

I chuckle. "I hid it on the floor of the backseat."

"I had no idea."

"See, you're not the only one full of surprises."

"How does it work?" Brandon asks, and I look at his big curious blue eyes.

"Well, it works like a real oven, but it's made for kids, so they get to bake but don't risk burning themselves with a real oven."

"I want to bake," Casey says.

I ruffle his hair. "Good. I'm going to teach you how."

Cason still hasn't come into the kitchen. He continues to watch me from the doorway, and my heart still in my throat continues to pound. I can barely catch my breath as he watches me with warm, appreciative, yet fascinated eyes, like I might have just solved world hunger. The Easy Bake Oven won't do that, but wow, I do love the way this man looks at me. It teases me in ways that makes me think he might want more.

"Are you going to join us?" I ask Cason and he takes a step closer. My breath catches simply from the way he moves. He gets closer and his warm scent washes over me. He steps behind me, his fingers trailing over my lower back, telegraphing a secret message between lovers. He likes this, and he's going to make sure he shows me how much later.

I can't wait.

"What do we do?" Brandon asks.

"Have you baked before, Brandon?" I ask.

"I made cookies with Mommy."

"Can we make cookies?" Casey asks, his big eyes wide. My heart almost hurts as I look at his cute, eager face.

"Is cake okay?" I ask.

Casey nods. "I like cake."

"How about chocolate icing?"

"I like chocolate icing," Cason says and I get the sneaking suspicion that it's not the cake he wants iced up—it's me. There is nothing I can do to suppress the hard quake going through me and he grins, knowing very well why.

"I'll let you lick the beaters then."

"I want to lick the beaters," Brandon says.

Casey climbs onto a chair. "Me, too."

"Okay, you boys can have the beaters," Cason says as he looks at me, his eyes indicating he has much more interesting things to lick.

"Okay, let's get started," I say. "First we wash up. You boys run to the bathroom. Use lots of soap. I want squeaky clean hands when you get back."

They dash to the bathroom and my head spins as Cason pulls me to him in a fast tug, aligning my pelvis with his. "I can't believe you did this!"

I shrug and look at the old green oven. My insides are alive, my thoughts jumbled as he gazes at me with heat, and something that might possibly be....love.

Do I dare hope?

"You said you always wanted one. I thought this would be fun. I don't know if it will turn out all that great with the bigger mix, but it should be okay, and I hope you like choco-late. Actually who doesn't like chocolate, right?" A wobbly grin tugs at the corners of his mouth as I ramble. Oh God, what is he thinking? "What?" I ask.

"You're kind of adorable."

I let loose a relieved laugh. "That's better than what I thought you might be thinking."

"What did you think I was thinking?"

I glance at all the supplies. "That you might think I was a big dork."

His big belly laugh curls around me. "Well maybe a bit, but did I tell you I liked dorks?" Before I can whack him, his mouth closes over mine for a warm, deeply passionate kiss that makes me forget there is a world beyond him, beyond this moment. But I'm quickly reminded when I hear two sets of feet pounding toward the kitchen. I break the kiss, and work to find my breath as we part, but he doesn't go far. No, he stays so close to me, a terrible distraction as I open the cake box and reach for a bowl.

"Okay, who wants to pour the mix into the bowl?" I ask the boys.

As Casey pours it and I measure out the water, Cason

produces a glass of wine and hands it to me. "I believe white goes with chocolate," he says, that same intense look on his face again, one that tells me exactly how he plans to taste his chocolate.

My hand almost shakes as I gratefully take it from him, take a sip, and set it on the table.

"How does a lightbulb cook it?" Brandon asks as he pours in the water, and I give Casey a big spoon to stir it.

"Well," Cason begins and goes into explaining how the heat from the light bulb can cook the cake.

I grin. "It's almost like you've done your research."

"I know things," he says like a four-year-old.

I laugh and put my hand on his chest. "Oh, I know. You're pretty and smart."

"Guys aren't pretty," Brandon says.

"Wrong," Cason says. "Guys can be whatever they want to be. If they want to be pretty, they can be pretty." I eye him, so proud of his values and acceptance of everyone, regardless of the color of their hair, piercings, or choices in life. He is such a sweet guy.

"I want to bake cakes," Casey says.

"Then that's what you should do," I tell him and hand him the beater. It's big in his hand, so I help him hold it, and soon enough, I give Brandon a turn. It's easy to tell how much they're enjoying this whole process by the looks on their faces, although they could just be excited because the end prize is, you know...cake.

Once they finish mixing, I remove the beaters and hand one over to each child. They eagerly lick them. "No eggs, no worries," I say to Cason.

"Not worried," he says, and I like how much he trusts me.

"This is yummy," Casey says and I take the batter and pour a bit into each tiny tray.

"Do we each get our own cake?" Brandon asks.

"Yes," I tell him and his eyes light up.

"Mommy would never let me eat a whole cake."

"Just don't go telling your mother you ate a whole chocolate cake. She'll kill me," Cason says with a laugh.

"Tell her it was a tiny cake and she won't mind." I slide the cakes into the oven, and the boys keep their eyes glued to the little screen as the lightbulb bakes it.

"I think they really enjoyed that."

"But you didn't get to play," I say and raise my wine glass to my mouth. "I'm happy to have the boys here and I love their fascination, but I wanted you to play with it, too." I take a mouthful of sweet wine.

"After they go to bed I'll play with it," he says and I nearly choke.

"Are you okay, Aunt Kinsley?" Brandon asks with a frown. My heart melts a little with his concern. He's going to grow up to be a wonderful man like his father and his uncle and I'm trying to focus on that more than on the fact that he called me his aunt, and it's possible that's the sweetest and scariest thing I've ever heard. I'm their aunt, sure. But for how much longer?

Cason steps away to grab a beer, and with my heart pounding a little harder, I rip into the icing sugar and grab the cocoa.

"Who's ready for the icing?" A strange groan crawls out of Cason's throat and I whack him and turn to the boys.

"Me, me," they both chant in unison and I laugh at the chocolate all over their faces. I don't think they'll be winding down anytime soon after all this sugar, but that's okay. I'm enjoying my time with them and plan to take advantage of every second of it.

We all work together on making the icing, and soon enough the Easy Bake Oven beeps indicating the cakes are ready. I carefully take them out and turn them onto a baking sheet, a little surprised that Cason's cottage is so well equipped, but guessing the other women had something to do with it. I do like how they all take care of one another here. It's also really sweet and supportive that they all want to come to the reception in my parents' garden. Personally, I'm dreading it.

After letting the cakes cool, the boys generously spread the icing. The second they're done, they're digging into them like they've been living off rations and I smile, so happy that I kept this old toy.

Once they devoured every morsel, I send them back to the bathroom to get washed up and I check the clock. "How about we all settle in for a movie, and get them to wind down after all that chocolate?"

"Great idea," Cason says. "I have a few here from the last time they stayed over."

"I think it's great that you spend so much time with them."

"I'm on the road so much, I don't get to spend nearly as much time with them as I'd like."

"Is it hard for the guys, hard on the relationships, being on the road all the time?"

"They find a way to make it work. Right now, with Khloe being so young, Katee travels with Luke. It was easier for Nina. She can write anywhere, right? But for those with careers keeping them in place, and when the kids are of school age, it can be a bit harder."

"So you think long distance relationships can work?" I ask, and he nods.

"Seems to for these guys. It might not be for everyone though."

I put the dishes in the sink and follow him into the living room, wondering if he could do long distance. He roots through the movies and pulls out a classic. "Just that if I were married to you, well technically I am, I wouldn't want to be away from you for very long."

I smile, but my heart is bouncing around inside my chest like a rubber ball. "Well, we are still in the honeymoon stage."

He chuckles. "You know that lasts for two years, right?"

I angle my head and eye him. "What? Why would you know anything about that?"

"My sister is a romance writer." He rolls his eyes. "She loves to fill me with all these facts I never need to know. But according to her, the honeymoon stage lasts for two years, then the deeper relationship really develops, and that can be a make or break point for couples."

"I guess it's not like we'll ever have to worry about that. We're on a deadline, right?" I say. Why did I pose that as a question?

Oh, because you want more, Kinsley, and you want him to say he does, too.

He frowns, and opens his mouth like he wants to say something, but I'll never know what it is, because just then the boys come racing back into the room, hyped up on sugar, and eager to go.

Cason pats the sofa and they plop down between us, and I angle my head to see Cason. His brow is still furrowed, worried lines around his mouth. What is going through his head? Did my question scare him, make him run the other way, his usual reaction as we close in on the two-week mark? Or is it possible that he was going to challenge that deadline, tell me he wants more? God, I need to know. I really, really need to know.

Then open your mouth and ask!

17

CASON

"You, my sweet wife, look amazing."

Fuck, man. I love calling her that and want to continue calling her that long after our thirty days are up, which are closing in on us quickly. As she stands in front of the mirror in my bedroom, she scrunches up her nose in concern and turns left and right, looking herself over.

"We're just setting ourselves up for disaster, Cason. Nothing good can come from this."

I shrug, but I'm not dismissing her worries. I understand them. "I don't know, maybe they'll see that inner light inside you glowing like I do, and realize you're doing exactly what you're supposed to be doing."

"They'll never approve of me choosing to be a chef over a lawyer," she says.

Okay, what I was getting at was her choice in a husband, but that answer will do, for now. We can talk about that choice when the night is over. It's well past time the two of us had a sit down and a serious discussion, because no way can I quit this girl. She's everything I ever wanted and never knew.

We've already made it past the two-week mark, heck we're actually almost finished with our third, and man, I've got it so bad for her. I've never in my entire life felt this way before. Never let down my walls with any woman.

"Hey," I say and put my hands on her shoulders. I spin her until she's facing me and drop a kiss onto her forehead. "I will not let you out of my sight. I promise. Let's go and show them how happy we are, eat some food, drink some wine, and then get back here so I can take this dress off your gorgeous body, and put my mouth all over you."

"Well, when you say it like that, what's a girl to do?"

I smile, and she lifts her chin to me, offering me her mouth. I cover her lips with mine, once again messing up her perfectly applied lipstick. I moan into her mouth, and break the kiss before I get a boner.

"Do you think my hair is okay?" she asks. "Maybe I should have put it up."

"Maybe you should just leave it the way you like it best."

"You're right. You're always right."

That's news to me, but one thing I am right about is this woman and what she means to me. No more screwing up, no more saying the wrong thing and fucking everything over. With her, it's so easy to be myself and say all the right things, so easy to open myself emotionally, because in my heart I know I'm not going to hurt her and she's not going to hurt me.

"Let's do this," I say and put my hand on the small of her back to lead her outside.

"Do you think everyone will show up?" she asks.

"Of course, they will. They'd do anything for us."

"I don't want them to be uncomfortable."

I laugh. "I'm sure some of your parents' friends watch hockey, and the guys will be a big hit. I guarantee it, and that will take some of the pressure off you." I frown and ask, "Do you think they'll be upset that I didn't ask my parents?"

She swallows hard and the sound travels. "It's best not to involve them, right? Isn't that what you said?"

I search my memories, but can't really remember. "Ah, yeah," I say. Honestly, I wish I had invited them. I want them to get to know Kinsley, and her asshole parents. They should at least know the parents of their daughter-in-law. Especially if I can convince her to be mine forever.

I open the car door for her and she slides in. I drop a soft kiss onto her forehead, not wanting to mess her lips up again, and she smiles up at me. My fucking heart swells in my chest. Jesus, I'm so crazy about this woman.

Her eyes are latched on mine as I circle the vehicle and climb in. Her hand searches for mine as I negotiate through traffic and in no time at all, we're at her parents' place. I pull behind Cole's car and smile. He usually takes it out when he's going to events, and maybe he's driving it tonight to flaunt it in my face, tease me with something he doesn't think I'll ever win.

He told you not to fuck it up with Kinsley.

Yeah, he did and that still confuses the hell out of me.

"Are you okay?"

I turn to Kinsley. "Yeah, why?"

"You're looking at that car the same way you look at me."

"How's that?"

"Like you want to make love to it?"

I laugh at that, but she's right about one thing. I do want to make love to her, and the sex between us is so good because there is love involved. She has to feel it, too. I mean she said make love over sex, right? With a burst of hopefulness inside me, I tease, "It is a pretty nice car, Kins."

She laughs. "Any other fetishes I should know about

before we go in there, husband? I am supposed to know everything about you."

"You will tonight, and the things I'm going to tell you are for your ears only. Our business, no one else's."

She goes quiet for a moment, and I can almost hear the wheels spinning. For a second I think she's going to call me out, and ask me to tell her right now, but instead she says, "Okay." I'm grateful, because I want to do it after the party, when we're alone at home.

Home.

I almost snort. I've always lived in a house, even growing up. It wasn't filled with laughter and dinners around the table, all the things Nina has and involves me in. She even decorated my house and cottage, wanting me to experience the warmth of home and hearth, but until I accidently found myself in bed with Kinsley, and we stayed in each other's lives and houses, I never knew what home really meant. I want to have a home with her. I want to have it all with her.

She exits the vehicle and I climb from my side and put my arm around her back. Voices from the backyard reach our ears, and I shake my head.

"What?"

"Sounds like Liam is the life of the party."

"We need to get that guy a girl," she says with a laugh.

"He doesn't need any help getting the girls. That's the problem."

She nods. "I know, and I know he's been through a rough time. What he needs is to meet his match, and fall in love and settle himself down."

"I agree, but I don't think Emily was right for him."

We walk into the backyard and I take in the gorgeous gardens all decorated with flowers and lights, candles, and chairs draped in fabric. There's even a banner with our names on it.

I put my mouth close to her ear. "They went all out."

She waves to Emily, who is chatting with Quinn and Jonah. Liam is standing near the bar, knocking back the drinks.

Emily is about to come over but stops when Kinsley's parents head our way. Kinsley stiffens beside me and I give her a reassuring squeeze.

Her mother plasters on a smile. "You look lovely, dear," she says, her gaze moving down Kinsley's dress, stopping around her stomach, like she's checking for a baby bump before she presents us to the crowd. "Many of your friends are already here."

"Yes," her father pipes in. "I met Quinn, she owns a daycare, and Jules is a nurse. Such great professions." His smile widens, "And Cason, you didn't tell me your sister was a New York Times Bestselling author. Now that's something to be proud of."

"I am proud of her," I say.

Lilith looks around me. "Are your parents coming?"

"No, they weren't able to make it. They give their apologies."

Once again, Kinsley goes tight beneath my palm, and I cast her a quick glance, but she doesn't look my way. Christ. Was it something I said?

Don't fuck this up, dude.

"Kinsley, you should know, Evan is here."

Her head jerks back. "Why would Evan be here?"

"To congratulate you two, of course," her father says, but her mother casts me a quick glance and I read everything in it. Do they seriously think she's going to drop everything, me included, and go back to a douchebag who dumped her when she no longer fit his agenda? My God, who are these people?

"How about we go say hello to Evan, then? Let him congratulate us."

Her parents both look surprised by my reaction. But I thought let's just face this head on and show them once and for all that Kinsley is with me and we're happy. We cross the gardens, stopping to say hello to a few of their friends, and most seem genuinely happy for us.

We catch up with Evan who has been talking to Liam, and an uneasy feeling sinks to the pit of my stomach. Judging by Liam's stance, he's had one too many drinks. I give a fast glance around and spot Cole. He instantly reads my distress and takes Nina's hand and makes his way toward us.

"Arthur, Lilith," Evan says, and I almost laugh as he uses their first names, a privilege I wasn't given, nor want—not until they start treating their daughter with the respect she deserves anyway. He turns to Kinsley. "Hey Kinsley, how's the food truck business?"

She stands a little straighter. "It's going well."

"She'll be expanding soon, starting a new restaurant in downtown Seattle," I say, and she tightens. She's worried about the space, but she doesn't have to be. It's hers. With or without her trust fund. It's hers.

Evan slowly turns my way, a smirk on his face. "So this is the infamous Cason Callaghan."

He throws his arm out for a shake and as much as I don't want to, I extend mine. "I wouldn't say infamous."

"Oh, that's not what your buddy Liam says."

The unease in my stomach expands, presses against my lungs, until breathing becomes difficult.

"Hey Liam, there's something I want to show you," Cole says, throwing his arm around him.

"Wait, you're Cole Cannon, right?" Evan says.

Cole straightens. "Yeah, that's me."

"Liam here tells me you're the owner of the 69, Dodge Hemi Coronet out front. That's a sweet ride you have," Evan says and tips his glass toward the front of the house, where we're parked.

Liam pales. "Ah, wait." He runs his hand through his hair and tugs.

"Oh, I'm sorry, Liam. I didn't do a proper introduction. I'm Evan Bateman. Kinsley and I go way back. Isn't that right Kinsley?"

Liam swallows. "Shit. You're her ex."

Shit is right because something tells me Liam didn't keep his mouth shut.

"What is going on?" Kinsley asks, and I put my arm around her.

"Come on, we should go," Cole says to Liam, his fingers curling into fists.

Liam nods, guilt and worry all over his face. He fucked up and he knows it. "Yeah."

"Don't run away," Evan says. "Not when we're all just getting to know each other."

"You're not anyone I want to know," Cole says.

"Want to bet?" Evan asks with a smirk.

"Back off, Evan," I say.

"Cason, what's going on?" Kinsley asks again.

"Aww, she doesn't know, does she?" Evan asks.

"Doesn't know what?" she says.

"Kinsley, we'll talk about it later. Why don't you go with Cole and Liam. I'll deal with this."

Evan laughs. "Tough guy, huh?" He snorts out a laugh. "You didn't have to marry a thug to get your trust fund, Kinsley."

"What is this?" her father asks. "You married just to get your trust fund?" He shakes his head. "I told you, Lilith. I told you there was something suspicious about this sudden Vegas wedding."

Kinsley's face pales. "Dad wait, it's not like that."

"It was a sham of a marriage. They planned to get it annulled after thirty days," Evan says.

Liam bends forward and practically sobs, as the truth comes spilling out. "Fuck, fuck, fuck," he chants.

"Consider your trust fund dissolved," her father says. "Unless you want to get your life on track again."

"My life is on track, Dad. I've never been this happy."

Shit, man, this is going south fast. I need to do something. I need to fix this.

"You could have married me, Kinsley." Evan says. "But now it looks like you don't get your money at all. What a shame. Unless you want to make things right with me, and join our firm. Come back to where you belong."

"You want *me* to make things right with you?" Anger flares in her eyes. "You were the one who kicked me to the curb, remember?" He opens his mouth to speak and she continues with, "And really you did me a big favor, Evan. I thank you for that." She puts her arm around mine. "This is the man I love and want to spend the rest of my life with. The man who respects my choices." My heart jumps into my throat as she confesses her feelings, and deep inside I know none of this is for show or to prove herself. She loves me as much as I love her.

"Maybe you'll thank me for this, too," Evan says. "You think he loves you? Think again. Your thug here had a side bet with his buddy, Cole."

A tortured sound crawls out of Nina's throat and she puts her arms around her husband to hug him—offering him all her support, but that's not what I'm getting from Kinsley. No, she's backing up and the look I'm getting would freeze the entire state of Florida, in the dead of summer.

"Wait, stop. It's not like that," I say quickly, trying to tug her back. "You don't understand."

"Cason," she says, her voice shaking. "The bet you had

with Cole was about me?" She blinks and looks down for a second, like she's searching her memory banks. "What was it you called it when I asked?" Her head lifts. "Oh yeah, I remember now. You called it a *stupid* bet." She jabs her thumb into her chests. "I'm the stupid bet?"

"Kinsley, wait."

"No, you wait. You said something about six months. What was that? What did that mean?"

Fuck me twice.

"Answer me, Cason. Honestly."

"If I didn't last thirty days with you, I couldn't have sex for six months, and if I did, I won his car. I'm sorry Kins, that sounds awful. Let me explain." I take a fast breath as she shakes her head no. "Kins."

She wobbles on her feet, her face so pale now, I'm sure she's going to be sick. She looks at Nina and Cole who are staring wide-eyed as they watch this fiasco unfold. "Did you know about it, Nina?" Kinsley asks.

Nina gives Cole an uneasy look and then says, "Yes, but Kinsley if you'll listen, let me explain."

"Listen!" she shrieks. "Oh, I don't think so. I'm not listening to any more of this bullshit." She looks directly at me. "I thought you were different, but winning a bet was the reason you stayed. I thought we moved past the sex and tacos, that you cared about me as a person, that I might have actually been special to you. But no. I was wrong. Fool me twice, right?" She gives a garbled laugh. "You were using me to get something. How are you different from Evan?"

"I am not Evan," I say, angry that she could even say such a thing.

She shakes her head, and almost to herself, she says, "This has all been a mistake, one that started when you crawled into the right bed with the wrong woman." Tears fill her eyes. "I should have known better than to let my heart get involved when all along I knew you thought you were with Emily that night."

"Wait, no. It wasn't like that. Well, I mean it was, at first, but then not." I take another fast breath and try to gather my scrambled thoughts but she doesn't give me time.

She points. "I want you all to leave. Right now."

I take a step toward her, and she moves back. Scowling at me, Emily puts her arms around Kinsley's shoulders and leads her into the house, away from us all. Asshole Evan comes closer, squares off against me. Oh, he's going to be playing the hero now, is he? Too fucking late for that.

"She asked you to leave," he says and tugs on the lapels of his coat, which fuels my temper even more.

"Fine, I'll leave, but this first." I pull my arm back and swing, punching him square in the face, and he flies backward. "That's for hurting Kinsley."

"Fuck," he says, from the ground. "I'm going to sue your ass off for this."

"I don't care. It was worth it." Before I go, I turn to her parents. "You might think Evan is the answer for Kinsley, but believe me, he's not. He hurt her, deeply. If you took the time to ask about it, you'd know. I know because I helped put her back together again."

"Oh, by staying with her for thirty days so you could win a car?" her father mocks.

"You don't know me, my life, or the reason behind that, so maybe you should shut up and listen for once." His eyes go wide and he glares at me, but I continue with, "Kinsley is an amazing woman. I'd like to think you both had a part in making her that way, and yes that's a compliment. But she's a grown woman now, who doesn't need to be judged for who she isn't, but for who she is."

Her father grunts. "And after this fake marriage you're telling me you know who she is."

"The marriage is real and I know who she is. She's a kind, generous woman who gives back to her community, and not from behind some desk making a token donation to look good on the books. She's out there with her hands every day, cooking and creating new programs to help the needy. She cares about others, and she cares about you two when neither of you deserve it. You need to make this right, before you lose her for good, and I'm telling you something, losing Kinsley doesn't feel very good." Actually, it feels like my heart's been torn from my chest and someone is still stomping on it.

Her father takes a step toward me, and I put my hands up. "I'll leave, but you two need to wake the fuck up and see what I see when I look at your daughter."

"Let's go, buddy." Cole puts his arm on my shoulder and leads me from the backyard. When we're away from the crowd, he shakes his head. "I'm sorry, Cason," he says. "The bet was my idea. I pushed it on you, thought I was actually helping and now everything is fucked because of it, because of me."

"I don't get it, Cole," I say, my voice cracking as Nina slides her arm through mine and walks with us. "Did you want me with Kinsley or not?"

"I wanted you with her so much, I was willing to part with my car." I shake my head, my brain too rattled to put the pieces of the puzzle together. "I knew she was the girl for you. I told you love would happen when you least expected it. I didn't want you to run away after two weeks like you usually do. I thought the car was incentive for you to stay for thirty days, so you could both explore your feelings and your relationship."

"I didn't stay because of the car," I say quietly.

"You stayed because you love her," Cole says.

I nod. "That's right." I tug on my hair, as my heart thunders. "Now she's lost her trust fund, probably her food truck, and definitely her restaurant."

"And you lost the only girl you ever loved."

"Yeah."

"Then what are you going to do about that, buddy?"

I lift my head, and as I stare at Cole, an idea takes shape, forms in the back of my brain. "I need to go to the cottage."

18

KINSLEY

"Why don't you take a break?" Kat suggests and my gaze jerks to hers.

"Why would I take a break? Do you see the line out there?" I bark back. She winces and I sigh. "I'm sorry, Kat. Just under a bit of stress lately."

"I can tell." She passes a taco through the window and starts on the next order. "For the last two weeks you've been kind of a bear."

"You're right, and none of it's your fault. I shouldn't be taking it out on you."

She takes the burrito bowl from me and sets it aside. "You shouldn't be taking it out on the food, either. You keep messing up the orders. No onion, remember?"

I swallow and wipe my head with the back of my arm. "Shoot. I can't afford to waste any more food."

"I'm sorry, Kinsley," Kat says as she starts a new burrito bowl, her eyes full of worry as she casts a glance my way. "I know things are tough right now, and I'm really sorry you lost the downtown space you wanted."

My throat tightens and tears pound against the back of my eyes. "When it rains, it pours," I say, working so hard to keep a positive attitude, but right after the 'wedding' party at my parents' house, I found out my dream space had been rented—snatched out from underneath me. Well, not really, since it was never mine. I lift myself up and straighten my shoulders. I'm not a quitter, dammit, and I have a positive attitude, despite the storm known as my life trying to drag me under.

"I'll find another place and another way to get it. We'll just have to keep this truck going for a little while longer, and maybe I can take on a roommate so I can save more." Just then the fridge makes an ungodly sound, and we both turn to stare at it. "Wonderful." I drop down, and pull open the door, to make sure it's still up to temperature. "I'm going to have to get someone in to repair this."

"I can ask my uncle. He's a handy guy and he probably wouldn't charge you very much."

I nod and stand back up. "You're sweet, thank you."

She passes the order through the window and turns back to me. "I can take over here. I already called Jason, and he's on his way to help."

My heart pinches. "Are you sure?" I ask, not wanting to put the lunch load on her, but I'm such a mess, I could use a fast break.

"Positive, now go clear your head and think about how you'd like to design your kitchen when you finally get one."

I reach behind my back and untie my apron. "Okay," I say, working to inject a bit of enthusiasm into my voice, but from the look on Kat's face, she knows I'm faking it. I'd drawn plans up once, and forgotten them at Cason's cottage. Not that they're of any use now.

"You look like you need a shoulder right now. I'd be that

shoulder, but I have to get these orders out. Can you call a friend?"

I almost snort at that. I gained and lost so many friends in the last month, my head is spinning. I loved being a part of Cason's tribe. Loved the women and kids and all the guys, and yet they were all conspiring against me behind my back. Well, not all of them, and the ones who were, I guess in the end they weren't my friends anyway and I need to stop thinking about them. I check my watch. Maybe Emily can take a few minutes and meet me for coffee.

The second I think of her, my phone rings, and I smile when I see it's her. I grab my purse, thank Kat again, and step outside into the sunshine. It does little to soothe my bruised soul. I slide my finger across my phone.

"Hey Emily, I was just thinking of you. Are you free?"

"I'm cheap, but I'm not free," she teases, and I appreciate her trying to put me in a better mood. She's been checking in with me for the last two weeks. Jules has called a few times, too, asking me to call Cason, give him a second chance. But I can't call him. He hurt me, far more than Evan ever did.

And why is that, Kinsley?

Because I loved him. Correction: I still love him. But I should do myself a favor and get over him. Wallowing in my own self-pity is absolutely ridiculous. I glance at the ring on my finger. Why the hell am I still wearing it, and why haven't I started the annulment process?

"Want to grab a coffee?" I ask, getting my head back to the present.

"Sounds great." I hear a male voice in the background, and for a second I think it's Cason.

"Where are you?" I ask. Maybe she has a male client that sounds like the man I'm in love with.

"Meet me at the market," she says instead of answering me.

I frown. Why would she want to go there, so far from her work? I don't ask, instead I agree and end the call.

Since the market is close by, I decide to walk, and I struggle to keep my thoughts on something—anything—but the man I haven't seen in the last two weeks. But that would be like stopping a freight train with my fist.

Speaking of fist…

I can't believe Cason punched Evan. Honestly, I can't believe all the things Cason said to my parents, standing up for me, right after he admitted he had a bet—a stupid bet—with Cole. Why would he do that, why would he stand up for me and say all those things if he was with me simply to win a bet?

Maybe that's not the real reason he was with you.

Oh, how I truly want to believe that, how I truly wanted to believe we were beyond sex and tacos, too. But if he wanted more, wouldn't he have wanted to introduce me to his parents? Wouldn't he have said something? Then again, I never said anything, either. I was too much of a chicken, too damn afraid of messing things up. Is it possible that he was, too? He told me numerous times he messes things up. Was he too afraid of saying anything and ruining what we were building? Should I have stayed in that yard and listened to him? Oh God, I just don't know what to think anymore.

What I do know, however, is Cason helped me when I needed it, was there for me at every turn, and stood up to my parents. He brought me into his circle of friends, and touched me with loving, tender hands. Would he have done all that if he wasn't one of the good guys, didn't care more about me?

"Earth to Kinsley." I blink as Emily waves her hand in front of my face, pulling me back to the present. I was so lost in thought I hadn't even realized I'd reached the market, standing on the corner as still as a statue, as people maneuvered around me. "Hey, are you okay?" She narrows her eyes and scans my face.

"No," I say, my voice low and shaky as panic wells up inside me. "I think I might have made a big mistake."

She eyes me for a minute. "You mean about Cason?"

I cross my arms and hug myself as the world spins around me. "I think I should have stayed on the lawn and listened to him."

She gives me a big smile, and it surprises the hell out of me. "Why are you smiling? You hate him. You told me many times how much you hated him for hurting me."

"Yeah, I know. Come on. Let's get a coffee and you can tell me all about why you thought you made a mistake." She puts her arm through mine and starts walking away from the market.

"Are we..." I jerk my thumb over my shoulder.

She doesn't look at me, instead she keeps her arm in mine as we cross the street. "Actually I heard about a new place that just opened. I want to try it out."

I shrug, not caring where we go, but there is an anxiousness inside my stomach. "Do you think I should call him?" I ask. "Do you think he'd even want to talk to me? I did say he was just like Evan. That was hurtful."

"That's because you were hurting." She gives my arm a little squeeze, and picks up the pace, her steps very purposeful. Maybe she's short on time, and has to get back to work. "You thought the worst, probably because of Evan."

We round the corner and my steps slow as we head down the street where I wanted to open my restaurant. I don't even want to walk by it, but Emily is dragging me along, giving me no choice.

"Maybe there was more going on with the bet than we

realized?" she says, casting me a fast glance before focusing on the street.

"Do you think so?"

"I do."

I eye her as I get the sense that something isn't right here. She's obviously had a change of heart where Cason is concerned. She was ready to neuter Cason and now it seems like she's siding with him. What does she know that I don't?

"What's going on Emily? What made you say there was more going on with the bet?"

"I think Cason can answer that better than me," she says as she pulls open the door to the downtown space I wanted to rent.

I go as still as a stealth soldier. "What are we doing here?"

She waves her hand. "It's the new place I mentioned."

"I don't think it's open." I glance up, but there is no sign over the door, and it doesn't look like any patrons are inside.

"It's open. Come on, let's check it out."

I shake my head. "I don't really want to."

"Maybe not, but you have to."

I have no idea why she's being so cryptic, and I don't get the chance to ask, because the next thing I know, she's hauling me inside with her. I'm about to turn and march back out when I find the place empty, but stop when my heart jumps into my throat.

"What...what..." I ask as I spin around. "This is my design. This is exactly how I drew it out when I was at Cason's cottage."

"I know," a very familiar male voice says from the kitchen area. I spin, and nearly sink to my knees as a very tired looking, very disheveled Cason comes from the back and makes his way toward me. The love I feel for the man overwhelms me as he closes the distance. He reaches me, and his warm scent fills the air, wraps around me like a comfortable blanket. It's all I can do not to throw myself into his arms. But I don't know if he wants that, and I don't know what the hell is going on.

"Cason," I say, as my brain races for answers. "What is this?"

"It's your restaurant." He shoves his hands into his pockets and glances around. "Just the way you wanted it."

I sink into a chair and put my hands over my eyes, as the world closes in on me. I shake my head and try to make sense of it all. "This isn't right."

"Did I not do it right?"

I open my eyes at the confusion I hear in his voice. "You did this? You rented this space?"

"I did."

I stare at him, dumbfounded as the tumblers slowly kick into place. "Cason, why would you do this?"

"Because you're my wife, and I believe action is stronger than words." He swallows. "You know I'm not always good with my words."

"You were with me," I tell him as tears pound behind my eyes.

Cason did this for me?

"There's a reason for that."

"What reason?" I ask, as my heart crashes against my chest.

"It's because you were right for me and I'm hoping I'm right for you." I open my mouth, but he puts his finger to my lips. "I fucked up. I have a habit of doing it. In the past, I think I was doing it on purpose, sabotaging those relationships when the girl I was with wanted more. I invented the two-week rule so we never got to that point again, because I never wanted to hurt anyone. I thought I was always saying the wrong things when it came to important matters, like my future. But really I was saying the right things, things that would end the relationship—

because in my heart I knew I couldn't have a future with any of those women. I wanted what all my friends have: the marriage, kids, minivans, but none of those women were right for me." My chest tightens, an invisible fist squeezing my heart as he continues with, "All this time the right woman was right under my nose." I blink through the tears, as he continues with, "Cole once told me love was going to happen when I least expected it."

"Love?" Oh God, is he saying what I think he's saying? My knees wobble, and my breath comes faster as he sinks to his knees in front of me.

"Yes, love. I love you, Kinsley. I love you so goddamn much and I'm fucking terrified that I ruined things between us. You were never a bet. Not to me. You were never just tacos and sex, either. You were and are everything to me. I'd move mountains for you."

"You love me," I say almost to myself.

A tortured groan catches in his throat. "Yes, Kinsley. I love you with everything in me."

I lift my head, and look at the gorgeous space. "You did this to—"

"To *show* you how much I love you. I mean, I didn't move a mountain—"

This time I press my finger to his lips. "But you did this in two weeks and that was probably harder than moving a mountain."

He kisses my finger and takes my hand in his. "I've been miserable without you. I can't eat or sleep, or even think, and the bet, Kins, it was wrong. Cole was pushing it on me, and I never knew why, but that's not on him. I took the bet, but helping you was never about winning his car. I promise you that."

"I don't understand. Why was he pushing it?"

"It was some fucked up way to keep us together. Nina was

in on it, too. They both knew how good we were together, and Cole was willing to lose his car to stop me from running after two weeks. He thought it was good incentive to keep us together, until I woke the fuck up, and realized you were the only girl for me."

I nod, my heart racing from shock and excitement.

I'm the only girl for him.

"I didn't need the incentive, Kins," he says and puts one palm on my cheek. "Marrying you was never a mistake. Nothing we did was a mistake."

"You...you thought you were sleeping with Emily."

He shakes his head. "No, I didn't. I admit, I did go to her room, but the second you spoke to me in bed, I instantly knew it was you."

My pulse does a cartwheel in my neck. "You did?"

"Damn right, I did. I was going to bail at first, because I was in the right bed with the wrong girl, and I didn't want sex to come between us. But the second you pulled me to you, I instantly realized I was in the wrong bed, but with the right girl."

My mind races back to that glorious night. "I thought I was dreaming," I say softly and because he's being so open and honest, I decide it's time for me to do the same. "I thought that because I dream about you, Cason. Fantasized, too."

He brushes my hair from my face, as his shoulders relax slightly. "I want to be with you Kinsley. I want to make all your dreams a reality."

"Cason," I say, and look around again. "This is too much. I just...can't accept all this."

"How is it too much?" he asks with a frown. "You're my wife, and a man is allowed to do whatever he wants for his wife, isn't he?"

I go quiet, and he doesn't even seem to be breathing as his eyes search my face, looking for answers.

"I made a mistake, Cason."

His body tenses, the hurt registering in his eyes bringing tears to my own. I touch his face, the bristles on his cheek rough on my palm. "I made a mistake when I said you were like Evan. You're nothing like him."

He lets out a fast breath that he must have been holding. "You were upset. I get it. But you are my wife. I don't care that it was a cheesy, Vegas Elvis wedding. You *are* my wife."

"Cason."

"Yeah."

"You're saying all the right things."

His smile is a little wobbly when he says, "If you'll let me, I'd like to spend the rest of my life saying the right things to you."

Tears spill down my face, my emotions on such a roller coaster ride, it's almost impossible to think straight. "I think I could get behind that."

Warmth races through me as he kisses my fingers again. "Am I the right guy for you?"

"You're the only guy for me," I say and he lifts me from my chair and spins me around. I squeal, my heart full of love and laughter. I take in my new restaurant as he spins me. My God, I still can't believe he did all this to *show* me how much he loved me. He really is one of the good guys, and I'm the luckiest girl in the world.

He sets me back on the chair and goes down on one knee. "You wanted something special, Kins. You wanted something just between us that we've never done with anyone else." He takes my hand, and asks, "Will you stay my wife?"

I laugh. "I can't say anyone has ever asked me that before." He smiles at me, and while it might be impossible, I fall a little more in love with him. "Yes, Cason, I'll stay your wife."

His smile is so big, he reminds me of a child on Christmas morning. "Then how about we christen this place, Mrs. Kinsley Elizabeth Palmer-Callaghan?"

"That's kind of a mouthful, Cason."

He grins at me. "Speaking of a mouthful..."

EPILOGUE

One month Later

"I am so nervous," I say to Kat as we take a peek out into the dining room.

"Don't be," Kat says as she ties her apron around her waist. "This is going to be a fantastic opening."

"That's right, Kinsley," Jason says. "Kira said we're almost completely full tonight."

I turn to look at Jason. "Did she now?" I tease, knowing full well he has a crush on the hostess.

"What?" he asks and squares his shoulders as he goes back to his prep work. "It's what she said."

I chuckle and look out into the dining room, and my nerves jump. I check my watch and nibble on my bottom lip.

"Don't worry, he'll be here," Kat says and nudges me.

I laugh. "I hate that I'm such an easy read." Truthfully, I know Cason would move a mountain to be here on opening night, but his practice has to come first and if they run late, there is nothing he can do about that. While I want my husband—I will never get used to saying that—I totally understand he has to work, too.

Just then Katee, Quinn, and my sister-in-law, Nina, all

walk in the door together, and my heart jumps, thrilled that they are here to support me tonight. My in-laws follow behind them and I wave. Cason introduced me to them right after I agreed to stay his wife, and I am lucky to have such great friends and family, but I'm sad that my own parents haven't talked to me since the backyard fiasco, and probably don't even know about this place. But I can't think about that right now, not when a beep lets me know our first order is in.

"Okay, let's do this," I say and we all turn our focus to making the best damn food in Seattle.

As the three of us work, and what an amazing team we make, a new set of footsteps on the kitchen floor reaches my ears. I turn to find Cason coming toward me, a huge smile on his face.

"Hey, babe," he says.

"You're not supposed to be back here," I tell him, as I go up on my toes for a kiss.

"I should leave then?"

I chuckle. "Not before you kiss me."

His lips find mine and I'm sure I just heard Jason say, "Get a room," under his breath.

"How are things going?" Cason asks as he rubs my arms and glances around.

"Fantastic. I can't believe this is really happening. I almost want to pinch myself, to make sure it's not a dream."

Cason reaches around me and pinches my ass. I yelp. "Not a dream," he teases and nods toward the dining room. "Half the team is here and we're all hungry."

"It's so nice that they're here to support you, Cason."

"They're here to support you, Kins, not me."

I smile, and lean into him, but then his face changes, his smile drops as concern dances in his eyes.

"What's wrong?"

He rubs my arms again. "I didn't come here alone."

I stiffen, having no idea what he's talking about. "Are you telling me you brought a date to your wife's opening night?"

He laughs. "I guess you could put it that way. Two dates actually."

I put one hand on my hip. "What's going on?" I ask, not at all worried my husband is hanging out with any puck bunnies. I trust him with every ounce of my being.

"I'm actually not sure if this will upset you or not, but..."

Worry weaves its way through my veins, but in my heart I know my husband would never do anything to hurt me, not purposely. "Cason, what's going on?"

"How about instead of telling you, I show you?"

"Okay," I say and he takes my hand in his. He leads me into the dining area and the buzz of conversation falls over me. I wave to my friends, and glance around to take in all the happy patrons, but my heart stills in my chest when my gaze falls on the couple sitting in the corner.

"Cason," I gasp, my hand going to my chest. He puts his arms around me. "Did you do this?"

"Yes and no."

Just then my father stands. Our eyes meet and the uncertainty I see staring back tugs at my heart. My gaze shifts to my mother, who looks just as unsure as my father. Are they worried I'm going to kick them out?

"I paid them a visit last week," Cason says. "I told them about your grand opening. I didn't force them to come, they wanted to." Tears fill my eyes, and I throw my arms around Cason. "Here's the thing, Kinsley. They treated you unfairly and manipulated you. You stayed strong and achieved your dreams. But the thing is, I think it's important to have our parents in our lives. They usually fix all the mistakes they made with us, with their grandchildren, and I want our kids to know them. I think it's important."

My legs are so wobbly it's hard to stand. I love this man, I love his values and morals, and the way he cares so deeply about those he loves, and I'm lucky to be one of those people. "You are the best husband ever."

He smiles. "I think we all have forgiveness in us, and I think them coming tonight means a new beginning for us all."

"You're right."

"Go talk to them."

I leave his arms and walk to my parents. I step up to their table and smile at them. "Thanks for coming," I say around the humongous lump in my throat. "What do you think?" I ask and spread my arms.

"I think we've found our new favorite spot," my dad says with a smile, and my heart swells. I glance at my mom, who is nervously toying with her napkin.

"Have you had a chance to look over the menu?"

She blinks up at me and in her eyes I see the love she has for me. "I thought we'd leave it up to you. Chef's special."

Tears press against my eyes. Calling me a chef is her way of apologizing, and I accept that.

"Okay," I say about to head back, but Dad's hand on my arm stops me.

"Kinsley," he begins and pauses. "You've got a fine man for a husband."

"He's the best, Dad." I glance at Cason, who is watching our exchange carefully. Ready to be there for me if I need him. "I'm a lucky girl."

"He's a lucky guy, too," he says and taking me by surprise, he puts his arms around me. "You did good, Kinsley. I'm proud of you."

A big stupid hiccupping sob rises from my throat, and Dad squeezes me tight. "Thank you," I manage to get out. He lets me go and smiles, but his eyes are damp, and that just about makes me cry harder.

"Now go wipe those tears and bring me some food," He

says sternly. "I'm starving. What do you have to do to get service around here?" I laugh, as warmth and happiness weaves its way through me.

"Yes, sir," I say, and he grins and sits back down. I smile at Mom and she smiles back, a new, deeper understanding and acceptance between us all. I turn to head back to the kitchen, but before I do, I walk back to my husband and I don't care who is watching, I give him a big kiss.

"What was that for?" he asks, grinning.

"For being the best damn husband in the world, and what you said earlier about us having kids, I thought we should get started on that tonight."

"Or we could right now. You do have a private office."

I chuckle. "As tempting as that is, I have hungry diners, and don't worry, I'll bring you lots of food." I wink at him and lust and love dance in his eyes. My God, I love the way this man looks at me. "You're going to need the energy for what I have in mind."

"Jesus, Kinsley, you're giving me a boner."

I grin. "Good," I say.

"And they call me the Troublemaker."

"There are some things you have no trouble at, husband," I say and a tortured sound crawls out of his throat as I saunter away, giving an extra shake of my ass to the ass man.

"You're going to pay for that," he grumbles.

I grin at him over my shoulder, all the love I have for him welling up inside me. "That's what I'm counting on."

AFTERWORD

Thank You!

Thank you so much for reading, **The Troublemaker**, book 8 in my **Players on Ice**. I hope you loved this story as much as I loved writing it. Keep reading for an excerpt of **His Obsession Next Door**, book one in my **Line of Duty Series.**

Interested in leaving a review? Please do! Reviews help readers connect with books that work for them. I appreciate all reviews, whether positive or negative.

Happy Reading,
Cathryn

HIS OBSESSION NEXT DOOR

"**W**hat's gotten into the puppies tonight?" Veterinarian Gemma Matthews asked her assistant as she finished securing the last howling pooch into its kennel.

Victoria gave a mock shiver and shot a nervous glance toward the shelter window. "It's the moon. It'll be full tomorrow night."

Despite the uneasy feeling mushrooming inside Gemma, she laughed at her assistant and followed the long column of silver moonlight illuminating a path along the cement floor. She reached the front lobby of her clinic, now eerily quiet after a demanding day of surgeries, and turned to Victoria. She gave a playful roll of her eyes, and said, "You've seen too many scary movies."

Victoria dabbed gloss to her lips, smacked them together and countered with, "Hey, it could happen."

Gemma arched a brow, humoring the young girl she'd hired straight out of veterinary college. "You think?"

"Sure." Victoria's long, blonde ponytail flicked over her shoulder as she gestured to the no-kill shelter attached to the clinic. "That's why the dogs are barking." Her green eyes widened and her voice sounded conspiratorial when she added, "They can sense the big, bad wolf out there, ready to shred a human's heart into a million tiny pieces."

"I hate to break it to you, Victoria," Gemma said, grinning at her assistant's antics, "but werewolves don't exist." Even though Gemma didn't believe in the supernatural, there was nothing she could do to ignore the jittery feeling that had been plaguing her all day. The truth was, the dogs weren't the only ones feeling antsy and out of sorts on this hot summer night.

Her assistant held her arms up and jangled the big, silver charm bracelets lining her wrists. "Well I'm not taking any chances, which is why I've armed myself with silver."

Before Gemma could respond, the office phone started ringing. As Victoria turned her attention to the caller, Gemma dimmed the lights and made her way to the front door to stare out into the ominous night. She stole a glance skyward and took in the mosaic of stars shimmering against the velvet backdrop. Even though the Austin night was calm, with not a cloud to be found in the charcoal sky, deep inside Gemma could sense a strange new ripple in the air. It left her feeling ill at ease. She placed a hand over her stomach, unable to shake the feeling that all was not right in her world.

Honestly, she had no reason to feel apprehensive or troubled, considering she finally had everything she ever wanted —her own clinic in the city, a no-kill shelter to help re-home animals, and an upcoming banquet that would hopefully raise enough funds to expand her animal sanctuary before she had to start turning pets away.

Swallowing down her edginess, Gemma set the deadbolt and was about to switch the sign from Open to Closed when a tall, dark figure stepped from the inky shadows. She sucked in a quick breath and felt a measure of panic as the very male, very *familiar* figure came into view.

Speaking of the big, bad wolf.

"Oh. My. God," she rushed out breathlessly.

"Is everything okay?" Victoria asked from behind the counter.

Instead of answering, Gemma's shaky hands went back to the deadbolt, certain she had to be hallucinating. The bell overhead jangled as she pulled the door open and the second she came face to face with the man from her past, the same man who'd rebuffed her seduction days after her seventeenth birthday, she feared nothing would ever be okay again.

Moving with the confidence of a man on a mission, he came closer, the long length of his powerful legs eating up the black sidewalk in record time. Even in the dark she'd recognized that hard body of his, developed from hardcore military training rather than endless hours in some sleek gym. Her gaze took in the leather motorcycle jacket stretched over broad shoulders before traveling back to his chiseled face. Dark, penetrating eyes—harder now from having seen too much carnage—locked on hers, and the raw strength of the impact hit like a physical blow.

He came barreling through her front door. "Gemma," he rushed out breathlessly. The urgency in his voice had the fine hairs on the back of her neck spiking with worry.

"Cole," she somehow managed to say around a tongue gone thick as she stumbled backward. "What...how...?" She choked on her words as she glanced past his shoulders to see where he'd come from. She'd been positive that after the funeral last year she'd never set eyes on this man again, and if she did, their chance meeting wouldn't go down like this.

Worried eyes full of dark concern cast downward. "Gemma...it's...it's Charlie...he's hurt..." Cole's fractured words fell off and that's when Gemma's gaze dropped.

Her heart leaped into her throat and she instantly snapped into professional mode when she caught the silhouette of the Labrador Retriever bundled in his arms. "Follow me." Jumping into action she turned and found Victoria rushing down the hall toward Exam Room 1, already a step ahead of them.

Gemma moved with haste and worked to quiet her racing heart. "Tell me exactly what happened." She kept her tone low and her voice controlled in an effort to calm Cole and minimize his anxiety.

Keeping pace, he followed close behind her, his feet tight on her heels. "We were out for a run in Sherwood Park," he began. "A squirrel sidetracked him, and he veered off the beaten path. He was jumping a log and didn't see the sharp branch sticking up."

She stole a quick glance over her shoulder and when dark, intense eyes focused on hers, her stomach clenched. "It's going to be okay, Cole. I promise." She drew a breath and gave a silent prayer that it was a promise she could keep. Gemma pushed through the swinging door and gestured with a quick nod toward the sterile examination table while she hurried to ready herself.

Understanding her silent command, Cole secured the whimpering dog onto the prep counter. Gemma's heart pinched when he placed a solid, comforting hand on the animal's head and spoke in soothing tones while Victoria went to work on preparing the pre-surgical sedative.

Gemma scrubbed in quickly and put on her surgery gear. She gave the dog a once-over before she dabbed at the blood to assess the depth of the wound. Angling her head, she cast Cole a quick glance. "Why don't you take a seat in the other room. This could take a while."

"I'm staying," Cole said firmly, their gazes colliding in that old familiar battle of wills.

Uncomfortable with the idea of him watching while she worked, and fully aware that he was a distraction she didn't need during surgery, she urged, "It could get messy."

"I've seen blood before, Gemma." With his feet rooted solidly, he folded his arms across his chest. "I'm not leaving him."

"Cole—"

"I'm fine."

Not wanting to waste time with a debate and knowing Cole was a bomb expert who'd seen his fair share of blood in the field, she gestured toward the chair in the corner. Once Cole stepped away, she cleansed the animal's wounds and continued her assessment.

She checked temperature, pulse and respiration before evaluating Charlie's gums. She shot Victoria a look as her assistant secured the blood pressure cuff and waited for the go ahead on the pre-surgical sedative.

"He's already trying to crash," Gemma said. "We have to go straight to surgery."

Working quickly, Gemma hooked the dog to an I.V. catheter and induced anesthesia while Victoria began the three-scrub process to shave and sterilize Charlie's skin.

Once the dog was clipped and scrubbed, Gemma reassessed. "He's lost a lot of blood, but I'm not seeing any visible organ damage. We'll have to flush the cavity to clean out the debris before we stitch."

As Gemma sprayed the area with warm saline, Victoria called out, "Pulse ox dropping, heart rate down to forty-five."

Damn, this was not good. Fearing she was missing something, she sprayed the area again and gave the cavity another assessment. That's when she noticed the tree had nicked a vessel on the liver. Gemma's heart leaped and worry moved through her as she exchanged a look with Victoria. Keeping her fingers steady and her face expressionless for Cole's sake, she worked quickly to tie the vessel off before it was too late. Once complete, she rinsed the area, and when the bleeding came to a halt, she exhaled a relieved breath.

She turned her attention to her suture. A long while later she glanced at the clock, noting that more than an hour had passed since Cole had first stepped foot in her door. Gemma secured the last stitch, wiped her brow and stood back to examine the dog.

"Vitals are good," Victoria informed her. Gemma gave a nod and took off her surgery garb. She quickly washed up and let loose a slow breath, confident that the dog would recover.

"Will he be okay?" Cole whispered.

Gemma's skin came alive, Cole's soft, familiar voice sending an unexpected curl of heat through her tired body. She turned to him and he stepped closer, the warmth of his body reaching out to her and overwhelming all her senses. As he looked at her with dark, perceptive eyes that knew far too many of her childhood secrets, she jerked her head to the right. "Let's go into the other room."

She pushed through the surgery doors and Cole followed her into the lobby where she could put a measure of distance between them.

"Is Charlie going to be okay?" Cole asked again, raking his hands through short, dark hair that had been cut to military standards.

Gemma rubbed her temples and leaned against the receptionist's counter. "He's lucky you got him to me when you did."

For the first time since stepping into her clinic, his shoulders relaxed slightly. "He's going to be okay?"

"Yes. He's going to be fine." She drew a breath and stared at the man before her, hardly able to believe that he was here in her clinic. Shortly after her botched seduction some ten years ago he'd enlisted in the army and had gone out of his way to avoid her.

As she considered that further, she decided to brave the question that had been plaguing her since he'd darkened her doorway. She waved her hand around the front lobby. "Why did you bring him here? There are other clinics closer to Sherwood Park."

Silence lingered for a minute, then in a voice that was too quiet, too careful, he said, "Because you were here, Gems, and I wouldn't trust Charlie's care in anyone else's hands but yours."

Her throat tightened at the use of his nickname for her, and while her heart clenched, touched at the level of trust he had in her, her brain cells made the next logical leap. "You've been back for a while, then," she stated in whispered words.

An expression she couldn't quite identify flitted across his face as he said, "A week now."

"Oh." Gemma shifted slightly, trying not to feel wounded that he'd been home for seven long days and hadn't even bothered to say hello.

She averted her gaze to shield the hurt but when he added, "I wanted to come sooner," she knew she could never hide anything from him.

She held her hand up to cut him off. "I understand how difficult this must be for you," she assured him, her mind going back to the last time they'd seen each other. Even though he'd been in a tremendous amount of pain at Brandon's memorial service, suffering as he said good-bye to his lifelong friend and fellow soldier, Cole had tried to console her, watching over her and taking care of her the same way he used to when they were kids.

It warmed her heart to know her brother hadn't died alone in the line of duty and that Cole had been there to care for him until the end. Her gaze panned his face. She took in the dark smudges beneath even darker eyes and couldn't help but wonder, who was taking care of him?

His eyes clouded as they stared blankly at some distant spot behind her shoulder. Hating the unmasked hurt on his face, as well as the awkwardness between them, she touched his arm. The air around them instantly changed. Cole flinched, his entire body tightening as if under assault. Gemma snatched her hand back, his rejection all too familiar. Even though she was all grown up now, a woman who wanted him as much today as she did all those years ago, he'd never see her as anything more than his friend's kid sister.

Just then the puppies broke out into a chorus of howls and Gemma couldn't help but wonder if they were on to something. Maybe the big, bad wolf did exist, and maybe she was staring at him. Perhaps she should heed Victoria's warning and arm herself with silver. There was no doubt that if she wasn't careful the man looming close could shred her heart into a million tiny pieces.

———

The second Gemma had touched his arm she lit a dangerous fuse inside him. Cole had immediately disengaged, knowing it could only end up backfiring and blowing up in his face. He hated the familiar hurt in her eyes when he recoiled, hated that he'd put it there—again—but he knew nothing good could come from the firestorm inside him, one that had been brewing since their youth. Gemma had tried to hide the pain, the hurt on her face, and she might have succeeded with someone who didn't know her the way he did.

"Gems," he whispered. He clenched his fingers and fought the natural inclination to pull her to him and comfort her like he did when they were younger. But if her body collided with his—one part in particular—she'd know how she affected him. And he couldn't let that happen. He had to stay strong.

Instead of acting on his needs, he took that moment to pan her pretty features, noting the way she'd tied her long, chestnut hair back into a ponytail. His gaze left her face to trail over the supple swell of her breasts as they pressed against her V-neck top. He shifted, uncomfortable as he perused her slim waist and the way her sensuous curves turned a pair of green surgery scrubs into a Victoria's Secret spread. Christ, she was even more beautiful now than she was when they were kids. But no matter what, and no matter how he felt about her, when it came to Gemma, there was a line he wasn't going to cross.

Her assistant came out from the back room. "He's stable and ready to go to ICU." When her words met with silence, her gaze tennis balled between the two, a sure sign that she felt the tension in the room every bit as much as Cole did. "Ah…Danielle will be here shortly. If you guys want to go, we can finish up."

Gemma exhaled slowly and pushed off the counter. "Thanks, Victoria. I'll come in early to check on him."

Cole stiffened. "He has to stay the night?"

"He needs to be monitored for at least twenty-four hours."

"Then I'm staying."

"It's not necessary. My night assistant will be here shortly, and I'm on call twenty-four seven. He's resting soundly and by the looks of you, you should be doing the same."

After a long moment, he gave a nod of agreement and Victoria slipped into the back, leaving them alone once again. Cole turned his full attention to Gemma and stretched his neck, working the night's tension from his shoulders.

Moving with an innocent sensuality, she walked around the counter to grab her purse from the drawer. Cole became fully aware of the woman standing before him and exactly what she meant to him. He shifted on his feet and tore his gaze away, looking for a distraction before his mind took him back to that hot summer night when she'd lured him into the barn nestled at the back of her old homestead. Christ, it had taken all his effort not to lay her onto the soft bed of hay and take what he wanted.

But at seventeen she was a kid, as well as the younger sister of his closest friend. Of course, those weren't the only things stopping him from acting on his urges. No, when his own parents had been emotionally absent—too busy looking for happiness in the bottom of a bottle—her folks had practically taken him in. Cole would never be disloyal to the family who'd treated him like a son by sleeping with their only daughter.

"It's late and it's dark. Why don't you let me walk you home," Cole said, breaking the uncomfortable silence hovering like the sharp blade of a guillotine.

In typical Gemma fashion, she straightened her shoulders in that old, familiar way that let him know he'd hit a soft spot. "I'm capable of walking home by myself." She lifted her head a little higher. "In case you haven't noticed, I'm all grown up."

Oh, he'd noticed all right.

She opened her mouth to say something else, but he countered with, "It's on my way, Gems."

That gave her pause. Her head jerked back with a start and he didn't miss the accusation in her tone when she said, "Let me get this straight, you know where I work *and* where I live?"

"Yeah," he said, for lack of anything else.

Her big blue eyes narrowed. "Why is it you know so much about me yet I know nothing about you?"

"What do you want to know?"

Without hesitating she asked, "If walking me home is on your way, where do you live?"

He gestured to the motorcycle parked at the curb outside. "For now I've got a cot in the back of Freedom Cycle."

Perfectly manicured brows knit together as she angled her head curiously. "You're staying with Jack?"

"You remember Jack?"

She nodded. "Ex-sniper. Brandon always liked him." At the mention of her brother she rubbed the back of her neck and a contemplative look came over her face before she began again. "When I moved into one of my parents' downtown apartments during college Brandon told me—" she paused to do air quotes before saying, "—*Jack of all trades* was my go-to guy if I ever needed anything. I've run into him a couple of times since the funeral."

Cole paused for a moment before saying, "He takes in ex-soldiers and gives them work until they get back on their feet again."

"What I heard..." Her voice fell off and her eyes widened. "Wait... Are you saying...?"

"Yeah. I'm getting out, Gems. My days serving overseas will soon be behind me."

"Oh," she said, a mixture of surprise and relief swimming in her big blue eyes. Then she frowned. "So you're sleeping in the back of his shop?"

"Just until my new place is ready."

"And when will that be?"

"Tomorrow."

"Where will you be moving?"

Gemma stifled a yawn, and Cole could see exhaustion pulling at her. Instead of answering, he said, "Come on, I'm taking you home." He tossed her a lopsided grin, one that always pulled a smile from her when they were younger. "You know, for old time's sake."

Their eyes met and everything in his gut told him her thoughts were traveling down the same path as his. She too was remembering her youth and all the times he'd taken her home and snuck her to her room so she wouldn't get busted by her older brother or her folks. Sure, he'd lectured her on the dangers of her rebellious nature, but he'd always had an inherent need to protect her, from everyone and everything. He couldn't bring himself to let her get caught, even though it might have been for her own good. Then again, as long as he was around and watching over her, no harm would ever come to her.

"Cole—" she began, but he cut her off.

"I know, I know. You're quite capable of taking care of yourself," he said to appease her protest. He still wasn't taking a chance with her safety now that she was living on her own in the downtown core and he was back from overseas. Besides, when Brandon was dying in his arms and there wasn't a thing Cole could do to save him, he'd asked only one thing of Cole. And no matter what, Cole planned to follow through with the vow he'd made to Gemma's brother on that dark night, because he never, ever wanted to fail Brandon again.

Confessions of a Bad Boy Fighter

Confessions of a Bad Boy Gamer

Confessions of a Bad Boy Millionaire

Confessions of a Bad Boy Santa

Confessions of a Bad Boy CEO

Hands On

Hands On

Body Contact

Full Exposure

Dossier

Private Reserve

House Rules

Under Pressure

Big Catch

Brazilian Fantasy

Improper Proposal

Boys of Beachville

Good at Being Bad

Igniting the Bad Boy

Bad Girl Therapy

Stone Cliff Series:

Crashing Down

Wasted Summer

Love Lessons

Wrapped Up

Eternal Pleasure Series

Instinctive

Impulsive

Indulgent

Sun Stroked Series

Seaside Seduction

Deep Desire

Private Pleasure

Captured and Claimed Series:

Yours to Take

Yours to Teach

Yours to Keep

Firefighter Heat Series

Fever

Siren

Flash Fire

Playing For Keeps Series

Slow Ride

Wild Ride

Sweet Ride

Breaking the Rules:

Hold Me Down Hard

Pin Me Up Proper

Tie Me Down Tight

Stand Alone Title:

ABOUT CATHRYN

New York Times and *USA today* Bestselling author, Cathryn is a wife, mom, sister, daughter, and friend. She loves dogs, sunny weather, anything chocolate (she never says no to a brownie) pizza and red wine. She has two teenagers who keep her busy with their never ending activities, and a husband who is convinced he can turn her into a mixed martial arts fan. Cathryn can never find balance in her life, is always trying to find time to go to the gym, can never keep up with emails, Facebook or Twitter and tries to write page-turning books that her readers will love.

Connect with Cathryn:
Newsletter https://app.mailerlite.com/webforms/landing/c1f8n1
Twitter: https://twitter.com/writercatfox
Facebook: https://www.facebook.com/AuthorCathrynFox?ref=hl
Blog: http://cathrynfox.com/blog/
Goodreads: https://www.goodreads.com/author/show/91799.Cathryn_Fox

Pinterest http://www.pinterest.com/catkalen/